W9-CGL-072

A PAGE OF MURDER

A SEABREEZE BOOKSHOP COZY MYSTERY BOOK 1

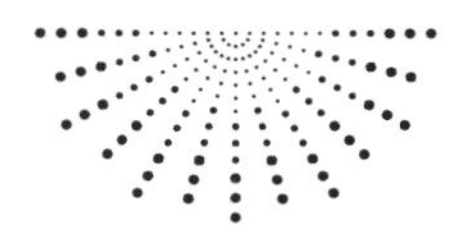

PENNY BROOKE

Copyright © 2021 by Penny Brooke

All rights reserved.

No part of this book may be reproduced in any form or by any electronic or mechanical means, including information storage and retrieval systems, without written permission from the author, except for the use of brief quotations in a book review.

This is a work of fiction. Names, places, characters, and incidents are either the product of the author's imagination or are used fictitiously, and any resemblance to any actual persons, living or dead, organizations, events or locales is entirely coincidental.

CHAPTER ONE

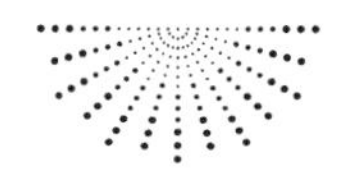

"Rue, I'm sorry, but I don't think I'll see you when you arrive."

My gran's words echoed in my mind as I pulled up to her house in Somerset Harbor, and a tinge of doubt coursed through my body. I know she'd told me that over the phone a couple weeks ago, but now, starting this new chapter in my life, I wasn't so sure this was my wisest decision. Had I made a terrible mistake? If only I'd known what was to come…

Okay, so trading my condo in Vermont for my gran's huge house with the wide front porch didn't seem like a bad deal on the surface. It wasn't like she was giving it to me. No, I was to look after it while she started her own new chapter in life—retirement, kicked off by taking her dream trip to Paris. On top of watching after the house,

I had signed on to manage her hole-in-the-wall book-store on the town's main strip.

Easy-peasy.

But, had I known what would transpire that fateful week I'd arrived, I would have never come. I would have respectfully declined this offer, but even so, I couldn't resist.

Set down by the sea a little south of Cape Cod, Somerset Harbor would be my new home—a town full of readers. Though people moved a little slower here, they were as full of purpose as anybody else—but not so full of the need to *rush*. The ever-present sea breeze and gentle lapping of the waves seemed to invite one to turn a page instead of staring at a screen.

So when my gran was ready to retire, I welcomed the chance to trade my sad attempts at selling real estate for a new career. I had more opinions, after all, on the best romance with elements of suspense than on whether a two-car garage brought more resale value than a water view.

Gran was now off to see the world; this was to be a year of new adventure for us both. Hers would be glorious, and mine would be terrifying. Although I didn't know it, the worst part of my story was just about to start.

Opening the back door to my Honda, my golden

retriever lunged out. It had been a long ride, and he was ready to run.

"Take it easy, Gatsby!"

My sneakers crunched below my feet as I strode toward the house, Gatsby now by my side. A smile formed on my face—this place was huge, and I couldn't wait to revisit it. I remembered spending summers here as a little girl, and now, in my early forties, just the smell of the nearby harbor wafting on the breeze brings me right back to those wonderful years running around the three acre property, collecting fireflies. Or relaxing on the porch swing.

I ascended the steps to the front door and pulled the welcome mat up. There lay a key—in this town, my gran could have left the door unlocked and nobody would have bothered with the place. The people here were friendly, and crime was practically non-existent…or so I thought.

Inside, I took a deep breath. It might have been my imagination, but I could smell the faint aroma of freshly baked croissants. My gran was quite the baker, and she favored French cuisine.

She and I had so much alike. Both about five foot two with sandy blonde hair and blue eyes. She had started dying her hair, not wanting to let the world know it was actually now snowy white, but at nearly eighty-five, she wasn't fooling anyone. Still, she was beautiful—my favorite person.

I brought in my luggage and made my way to one of the guest rooms. I plopped my suitcase on the bed and opened it. Gatsby oversaw my unpacking, and then after I was done, I went to the kitchen and fed him dinner.

"Are you ready for tomorrow, boy?"

Gatsby looked up and let out a huff.

Of course he was ready for our first day of work. I'd take him along with me, since the shop was pet friendly, like most shops on the strip. Not only that, my gran had insisted that I take him, since the last time I was in town, Gatsby seemed to attract everyone's attention, with his calming demeanor. He would be an asset at the store, she'd told me. Only time would tell if that statement would prove true.

I whipped up a quick dinner—lemon garlic salmon with a side of mashed potatoes and string beans. After devouring that delicious meal, I pulled on my pajamas and got ready for bed. I needed to ensure I was well-rested for tomorrow. It was going to be a big day.

The next morning, I arrived at the bookstore with Gatsby trailing behind. Already there was a mousy woman around my height, her dark locks drifting into her face. She sat behind the counter, looking bored as ever. How could a person be bored in a place like this? Scanning the little shop, I saw a couple thousand ways one could keep themselves occupied. Of course, as a part timer at the shop, this woman's job wasn't to get lost in a book, but to help any customers in the store—at the moment, there were none.

"Hi," she said, voice low.

"Hello there," I said, and shook her hand, which felt like a limp fish. "I'm Rue Collier. I'm the new manager. You must be Ellen."

"Yeah," came her reply.

My eyebrows rose at the second monosyllabic reply. This person had about as much personality as a clam, but hopefully I'd get her out of her shell.

"Where's Elizabeth?" I asked her.

Elizabeth was a longtime friend of mine, and I'd always wondered if she'd ever leave this town. At one point, my parents had moved here, and spending a few formative years here, Elizabeth and I had formed a bond. Even after leaving town, we stayed in touch.

Ellen shrugged, not even bothering to mutter a reply. Getting her out of her shell might be harder than I'd thought.

A few hours passed as I moseyed around the store,

getting reoriented as to where everything was. There were book tables that were featured staff picks, arranged by selected genres. There were also a few sale tables as well, but most of the store's offerings were on shelves. Every wall in the place had a shelf, and there were a couple rows of shelves as well that our customers could browse along. Genres were clearly labeled, and just like most bookstores, the books were categorized alphabetically by authors' last names. I scanned the store, ensuring I knew where everything was. It would take a few days to jog my memory of where everything was, though it would all come back to me—I'd helped out here many summers, and not much had changed since.

I approached the front counter and regarded Ellen. "You can take your lunch break now."

"Okay."

She shuffled past me and exited out the front door, the bells jingling above her. I took a seat behind the counter and waited for the first customer to arrive. A rustling noise came from somewhere in the bookstore, and I peered around. Nothing.

What was that? It almost sounded like it was coming from the top of one of the bookshelves.

I shrugged—just my imagination. But still, I knew I should have a quick look around.

I checked around the store and cocked my head. A few books lay on the floor. I could have sworn these had just been positioned on their sides on the nearby table. Who was even in here who could have knocked them over? We hadn't had a single customer all day.

I shook my head, unsure of what was going on. But I'd get to the bottom of it…

Returning to the counter, I sat back down and kept my ears open, but nothing else could be heard.

Fifteen minutes later, the bell jingled and in strode a woman around my age. She dressed athletically, like she'd been out for a jog, though if she was, she hadn't broken a sweat. Her blonde hair was pulled back in a bun, and the rosy hue on her cheeks barely hid the freckles on her face.

"Hi," I said. "Welcome to the Seabreeze Bookshop." Then my eyebrows rose when I recognized her. "Anna? Is that you?"

"Hi, Rue."

"It's been forever. How have you been?"

"Oh, you know. Living the dream."

"I bet. How's your bakery?" Anna owned Anna's Sweet Dreams Bakery, where gossip was just as much a staple as her to-die-for spice cake with maple cream cheese frosting. Since it was only next door, I knew I had to stop in on my next break.

"Staying busy, as always." She cast a glance over her shoulder, then fixed her gaze to mine, a look of worry on her face.

"Are you okay?" I asked.

"I'm fine," she said, then strode around the store, browsing.

A few minutes later, she was back at the counter, and her phone buzzed in her pocket as she handed over a stack of three paperback mysteries, each with a moody watercolor landscape on the cover. She pulled the phone from her pocket, then glanced at it, eyebrows scrunched. She tapped the phone furiously, and a bead of sweat sprung out from her brow. Then, she let out a huff and slipped the phone back into her purse.

"Are you sure you're all right?" I asked.

She stared at me for a long moment, looking white as a ghost. "Better now, I think." She was breathing hard. "I don't know what came over me. I just started to feel faint."

I ran her AmEx through the reader while Gatsby nuzzled a nose into her side to tell her things would be okay.

"I hope you're not getting sick," I said as I bagged her books. "Crawl into bed and read tonight; make sure you get some rest. I hear these are Rachel Thorne's best work." Anna had picked some of the first books by the only celebrated author our town had produced.

"Books in bed sounds good. Thanks, Rue." As she turned to leave, she bumped into a display of Staff Picks by the counter and bent down to get the books that had spilled out of her bag. Before I could point out that the ginger tea we sold worked wonders for a cold, she was out the door.

I watched as she scurried down the street and shook my head. She was really acting strange.

She was one of many who had made me feel a part of things here in Somerset Harbor, whenever I had visited and helped out in my gran's store. There were lots of regulars like Anna, who loved to linger by the shelf that held our books on France. It was a subject—*c'est magnifique!*—with which she seemed to be obsessed, along with my gran. Those two could discuss their obsession for hours. Of course, obsessions, the need to know, or longings for another place or time could flip the magic switch to turn browsers into buyers—my gran had told me that.

After Anna left, it was almost time to close, and two customers entered. A teenage boy and girl. They browsed around as I prepared to shut down for the night.

I sensed a shuffling near me, like someone was

approaching. But when I looked around, the two remaining customers were somewhat at a distance, browsing quietly.

It's happening again.

Gran had never mentioned ghosts, but this was the second time today I'd heard noises in places where noises shouldn't be. I'd even found those books toppled over.

Of course, I never *really* entertained the idea of a ghost. Perhaps it was Gatsby—of course! Even though he was the gentlest and most careful of big dogs, he could have easily jostled those books off the table and produced the rustling noises I had heard... But weren't those noises coming from the tops of the shelves?

Either way, it probably had been Gatsby. Perhaps my own clumsiness was rubbing off on him. Even Elizabeth had teased me about the way my head was always in the clouds. Hopefully, when she arrived to work, she would help me get to the bottom of this little mystery. And maybe help me overcome my own clumsiness.

I grinned. Despite my shortcomings, I'd finally been able to put my skills to good use. I'd spent the last ten years trying on professions, none of them quite right. Turns out, I'm like my gran and have a knack for matching books to readers. Like a ninja in the bookshelves, I could find the perfect read with a quick glance through the pages. With an almost uncanny knowledge of every book I'd ever read, I knew what every person in my life should pick up and read next. Over the summers I used to help out at the shop, a steady stream of customers came in eagerly for what I had to offer, and my gran had told me my gift was not a small thing. The right book could fix a lot of things. There were self-help books that said *you are not alone,* biographies that let customers keep company with the greats. The books on these shelves offered smaller gifts as well: something new to serve with fish or ways to organize your closet. I knew I was of value. And, really, when I think about it now, that was the true reason I had agreed to help my gran out and move to Somerset Harbor. For the first time in my life, I felt like I belonged.

"Um, excuse me, ma'am?" My thoughts were interrupted by the teenage boy, who wore a look of slight alarm and a well-worn Red Sox cap. Improbably, he held on to a gorgeous black and pink crossbody bag I recognized as Coach. I loved the classic snakeskin detail as he set it on the counter, but it hardly seemed his style, I thought with wry amusement. Most likely what we had here was an obedient boyfriend whose true love needed both her arms free for books.

"I think somebody left this," he said, looking worried.

"I just looked and saw it sitting here, right beneath the counter."

Anna's purse.

Oh for goodness sake. As if the poor dear's day had not been bad enough. She must have set her purse down when she bumped into the book display and spilled her bag. How had I not noticed a fine new purse like that when she took out her wallet? The counter sat up high, and she must have had the bag pressed against her hip.

I thanked the boy and took the purse, opening it up to check for an ID to be sure it was hers. Sure enough, in the plastic driver's license section of the wallet, there was Anna's picture. A huge smile was spread across her lightly freckled face with only one deep line on her forehead to hint at her approaching middle age. I was about to call her when my finger brushed up against something hard; it was Anna's cell phone.

Well, no need to call.

And I couldn't call the bakery number either. She closed at five on Mondays, and now it was almost eight.

As I put the wallet back, I noticed a text message still up on her phone, its screen still brightly lit.

Okay, okay, okay. I know what you're thinking! And I didn't mean to pry. But I've always been...well, *curious*. And sometimes by the time your brain says to be polite, your eyes have looked already.

So there were Anna's words highlighted in blue: *Leaving bookstore now. Feeling terrified. I don't want to be alone here. It's evil, pure and simple. Help! Not sure what to do.*

I felt two things at once: paralyzed by a cold knot of fear and confused by the odd message. Could it be that she felt threatened to be here in this sweet store? Surely not. With the bakery being just next door, the bookstore had become a second home for her. I remember my gran telling me that some nights after work, she'd come in to browse among the mysteries; other times she'd sit in the corner reading nook with some picture books on France. I'd heard that she always looked so peaceful and contented in the cushioned Book Nook with its billowy white and sea-blue curtains with silver stars pinned in the corners.

Someone beside me coughed, causing me to jump. Again, it was the young man. "Um, excuse me, ma'am?" He looked concerned. "I believe your cat needs some help?"

I smiled at him politely. "I appreciate your thoughtfulness—but I don't have a cat."

For the love of Shakespeare, could this day get more bizarre?

He stared at me, confused. "There's a cat up on the bookshelf."

I restrained my eyebrows from furrowing. Whose cat could this have been? This boy and the girl with him were the only people left in the store, or so I thought.

His voice broke into my pondering: "Maybe it belonged to the lady who left her purse? Do you think she left her cat as well?"

What? Did he think that people just went wandering around, shopping with *their cats?* At that very moment, I could hear the creature's terrified meows—along with the girlfriend's coos as she gazed up at it.

Oh, for heaven's sake, I thought, going for the ladder. The kitten, a British shorthair that was gray and very tiny, had somehow made its way up to the very highest shelf, reserved for earth science and astronomy. Both were worthy topics, but seldom was anyone required to pull out the ladder to fetch them off the shelf.

Well, one mystery was solved. I knew now what had happened with all the little spills and the shuffling noises when no one was there. As the weather had been gorgeous that day, I must have opened a window to let in the breeze. I guessed I'd also let something else—or *someone* else—inside.

I went for the ladder, and with the rescue completed, I let the young couple know it was time to close. "We'll take him outside with us," said the girl, cuddling the kitten to her chest. I could hear their voices on the porch a little later, hers insistent and his pleading. "A dog might be okay," he said, "but—please, please—not a cat."

I wasn't sure I agreed with him. Sure, I'd always had a dog—sometimes two and sometimes three—but I'd always wanted a cat. Part of me wished I had kept the kitten, but I'd already allowed the teens to take the beauty home—perhaps the boy had already warmed to the feline.

I shut both the windows, which I guessed would *stay* shut from now on. I'd miss the sweet breeze on my face as I went about my day. I walked through the store, turning out the lights.

The kitten had been a nice distraction to get my mind off of that text. I picked up my keys and purse along with Anna's bag, determined to find answers. I'd stop off at the bakery, hoping I could catch her working after hours. If not, she lived above the business, so one way or another, I'd make sure she got her purse. If I asked some open-ended questions about the bad day she was having, she might give me just a little hint of what was going on. If not, there'd be no way I'd get any sleep that night.

I'd love to think there was an explanation that would fill me with relief. Maybe I'd talk her into going for a late dinner to catch up, if she was feeling better. In truth,

I felt I'd be a little lonely when the bookshop closed that first night. I'd made a few friends here over the years, but most were busy with their families when they were done with work.

As I walked down the bookstore steps with Gatsby bouncing happily along beside me, I could sense that something wasn't right outside. Small groups were gathered near the cedar-shingled shops, although most of the businesses had been closed for hours. The voices were quiet, almost whispers. When I held my hand up in greeting, some of my acquaintances nodded solemnly while others simply gazed at the cobblestone below. Gatsby barked out his hellos, happily unaware of the odd sense of gloom.

Then bright lights hit my face, and streams of panicked blue and white beams flashed across the sidewalk. Someone began to wail. The knot in my chest tightened into a noose as a group of uniformed officers rushed past me with some other men. I recognized one figure who was a little shorter and much rounder than the others, though he didn't wear a uniform.

Is that...?

My eyes widened with realization. "Andy? Hey, hold up!"

Andy whirled around, his brown eyes open wide, winded with the effort of keeping up with the younger, fitter men and women. When they met mine, his eyes turned soft. "Oh, hey, Rue. Didn't realize you were here already."

"Just came in last night."

"I take it you heard..."

"Heard what?"

"Rue, I'm so sorry. I know you two were friends."

"What are you talking about, Andy?"

He put a gentle arm around my shoulder. "It's Anna."

"Anna?"

Andy nodded. "She's been stabbed."

I was afraid my heart might fall out of my chest. "She's been stabbed? By who?"

"There's not much that we know now. It just happened," he said softly. "I know this must be a shock. Why don't you let me drive you home?"

"Is she hurt very badly? Please tell me she'll be fine."

But his eyes had gone all dark with the thing I had already guessed. He watched the sidewalk closely, putting off for just a moment the words he didn't want to say. "I'm afraid your friend is gone."

CHAPTER TWO

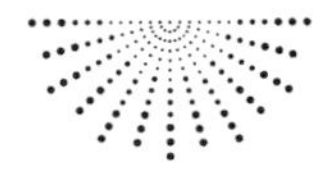

The next day, I was dragging after way too little sleep—my friend's death had kept me up all night. I'd checked her social media accounts in the early morning hours and learned that she'd been so full of plans: a hiking trip with friends; season tickets to the symphony with Renee, her sister. One minute, I was thinking I should give the cops the phone. They had to catch the killer, and that text had to be important. The next minute, my heart would nearly somersault out of my chest, and I'd stare down at the counter, paralyzed with fear.

There had been just one customer so far, Lilly from the gourmet kitchen shop, who came in to buy a gift. "From what I hear, the cops have absolutely nothing," she said. She browsed through my selection of fine pens and leather journals. "They have no leads at all, or at least that's what I heard."

Well, there was *one* clue, an odd one. It was locked in my desk drawer.

When Lilly was gone, I refreshed the homepage of the *Somerset Daily Press* and checked for messages from Andy, who had said he'd fill me in as soon as he knew anything. He was retired from the police force, but when something big was brewing, he still showed up on the scene if he was in town. It was a small department, and they could always use the help in the rare event of any kind of major crime. And from what my gran had told me, none of the guys they had now were half as smart as Andy. Now he worked as a private investigator, having set up shop in a small office down the street. "I'm too old to have a boss," he had told me once by way of explanation.

Without a magic password, I had not been able to dive in and find whatever secrets might be locked in Anna's phone. There were a million questions swirling in my mind. Was I safe inside my own store? Would I be a suspect in *a murder?* Because to some, that text might seem to point a finger straight at me.

Elizabeth breezed in around eleven, the gold and red

patterns in her shawl doing very little to brighten up the mood. Carrying a large box, she made her slow way to her corner of the store with its sepia-toned sign: *Curiosities and Antiquities by Elizabeth.* She heaved the box down on her desk then rushed over with a hug. "How you doing, sweetie? Tell me I did *not* hear the thing that I just heard." She let me go and brushed her graying hair out of her eyes. "This does not seem real. I just talked to her not that long ago."

"I just talked to her *last night*—right before it happened."

"Oh, Rue. That must have been such a shock." A crease formed on her forehead, and she suddenly looked every bit of her sixty-three years. "Did she give you any hint that something might be wrong?"

Oh boy, did she ever. With my heart pounding in my chest, I told Elizabeth the story, anxious to have someone help me figure out what the heck was up. Thank goodness that I had a friend I could trust with a thing like that. You can't just say to anyone, *Hey, I have a text that might implicate me in a murder. Should I hide it from the cops?* After I told the tale, complete with tears, I took a nice, deep breath. "Gran never said a word about any kind of…evil in the store. What did that text even mean? Bad karma? Evil spirits? Something hidden in the books? Oh Elizabeth, I'm just so confused."

Elizabeth shook her head. "There's never been a hint of trouble in the place. This is a *happy* store—and almost even sacred. Because—you know—the books!" A hint of pride showed through the sadness. "This is still a town where people give a place of honor to a book." She paused. "Could it have been a person who was maybe stalking her when she came in here, who followed her into the store?"

"She always came in after work when it was kind of quiet, so I don't *think t*hat's what it was." I stared out the window and watched a red bird resting on top of a street lamp. I knew I'd done the wrong thing. I should have told the cops last night that I had her bag, but I couldn't bring myself to do it.

Elizabeth gently grabbed me by the arm and steered me toward the curtained Book Nook, where we both took a seat underneath the hand-lettered message. *There is no Frigate like a Book To take us Lands away. Emily Dickinson.*

Lands away sounded really good.

"What you're in possession of is important evidence," Elizabeth told me gently. "And there might be other things that they need in her phone or in her purse." She paused. "And we want them to catch the person who did that to our Anna."

I knew she was right, but if I kept that bag in my

drawer, my new life here could continue smoothly. People wouldn't think some monster had blown into town to take over a beloved store. I'd loved the Seabreeze Bookshop even as a child when I'd come to visit Massachusetts. Gran would let me pick a book, and she'd turn the colored pages into a kind of party. For *The Very Hungry Caterpillar,* we'd prepared a feast: two cupcakes lined up beside two apples beside slices of watermelon beside a gooey chocolate cake. At the right moment in the story, we'd pause to each take a bite and munch along with the caterpillar.

Now as an adult, I'd finally found the place I was meant to be. There were stories everywhere, not only in the pages of the books, but in the photos, scrapbooks, and old letters Elizabeth brought in. Above her little nook was a string of delicate white lights on which she'd hung a selection of her latest finds. I gazed up at an eight-by-ten photo in a protective sheath. A woman with long silky hair and smoky eyes looked back with a smile. It was just a small smile, as if she was amused. But despite the smile, something in her eyes looked sad. In the background was a rooftop with a picture of a pig with wings.

Elizabeth saw me looking. "I thought she was gorgeous when I saw her. And you have to wonder—what's the story with that smile?"

"And with the flying pig," I said.

"There can be whole novels in single photographs. I see it all the time."

We each sat quietly, lost in our own thoughts. Then she broke the silence. "The thing that they don't know at Anna's bakery is that when we go out into the alley to take out the trash, we can hear them in the kitchen." She watched me for a sign that I knew where she was going.

I did not. "And what was it that you heard?"

"Well, there have been a few times that I've heard her and her new assistant, Jules, going at each other hard. It's been like my own personal soap opera going on next door."

"My gran had told me about Jules, and that Anna wasn't a fan of him. Said she wasn't sure why Anna put up with him. So, did you hear anything that they were saying?"

"Mostly I'd just pick up on their tone. It wasn't like I could hear whole conversations. But last week, things got heated. And that loser Jules was almost *yelling* at her. He called her selfish, Rue—and some other choice words that I won't repeat."

"You should tell the cops."

She couldn't help but smile a little. "Isn't that *my* line? But yeah, I'll let them know. Although I'm sure the others in the bakery know those two are at odds. It's really nothing new."

I reflected on everything my gran had said about Anna and her new assistant. In almost every way, Anna's assistant was the opposite of her. Jules was theatrical, and he was always pushing her to change up the menu or the way the shop was run. Anna was having none of that. She preferred to quietly go about her business in the way that had made her a kind of star. Anna's place had been a top-five bakery in New England for the past five years in *Edible Delights.* Now, Jules moved about the place as if that was all *his* doing. I'd sensed right away the guy was a jerk.

Elizabeth got up to pour some tea. "A cup for you?" she asked.

"That might be nice," I said. "Hey, listen, I was thinking. Do you think that Anna might have been afraid that Jules would come in the store to find her? There has to be a reason that she sent that text."

Elizabeth shook her head as she handed me the tea. "I've only ever seen her come in by herself."

"Plus, he wasn't here last night, and that's when something spooked her." I slowly sipped the tea, which tasted of green apples.

Elizabeth settled back against the cushion. "You know, where I see him the most is out there on that bench between our store and the bakery. I see him there a lot when I go home at night. He says he likes the quiet when the stores are mostly closed." She sighed. "It's kind of creepy, really."

I thought about the text. *Leaving bookstore now.* Perhaps it wasn't being *in* the store she dreaded—but walking past that bench outside. Had Jules been waiting there? *I don't want to be here alone.* I thought about that line as well. *Here* might be the space between my friend and the safety of her apartment. A scene unfurled in my head: *Anna reaches for her keys and sees her purse is missing. She turns to rush back to the bookstore. A hand reaches from the darkness...*

I remembered that sometimes Anna had hung out at the bookshop until right before it closed. Since we stayed open later than most of the neighboring shops did, she'd be stepping onto streets gone dark and fairly empty—except, perhaps, for Jules on his favorite bench. And since she lived above the bakery, he could follow her straight home. But it still made little sense. If she'd been scared of Jules last night, why not just stop by the bookstore after work and be home by dark?

I said all that to Elizabeth, who gave me a little shrug.

"I'm sure they'll look at Jules," she said. "In addition to the trouble between him and Anna, it won't help his case that he's new in town." She sighed. "You have to live here fifty years until some of the 'old guard' takes you in as one of us. Until then, they kind of watch you like you're just south of shady. And the cops, they are the worst."

"Well, that kind of stinks for me." I thought I might throw up.

"Oh, but you'll be fine." Elizabeth reached out to touch my knee. "You belong to Pamela; that means you're in the club. Your gran is royalty almost to some of the people here." She rubbed Gatsby's ears when he came to place his head on her lap, and we sipped quietly, gazing out at the quiet street. "Oh, and look, I know there's a whole lot on your mind, but really, Rue—a cat? A cat in a bookstore? Don't you think that's so cliché?"

"*So* cliché," I said. I rubbed Gatsby on the neck. "Dogs are the way to go." My gran's store was a place where you were always welcomed with unbridled joy—and sometimes puppy kisses.

"So what's up with the cat?"

"What cat?"

"Why, *that* cat of course." She raised an eyebrow at me, nodding at a box of unpacked bookplates in the center of the room. Barely visible over a cardboard flap were two white furry ears. The kitten watched us, startled, as if it had been us who'd popped in uninvited.

I put my cup down and sighed. "He was here last

night. He must have snuck back in with you or Lilly." We watched as he jumped out of the box and pounced playfully on a paperclip, which he batted at for several minutes. Then I went out for the mail, and he followed me outside.

When I walked back in, Elizabeth was in her section unpacking the big box she'd carried in that morning. The sense of dread, which had come in waves, washed over me again as my mind turned back to Anna. Of course, more than anything, I wanted justice for my friend. But I also knew I had to protect myself and my business. That text the cops would see—if I chose to show them—was just one part of the story, and you have to read the whole book to understand the plot. If all the evidence they had was Anna's phone, they'd zero in on me—the new girl, the outsider.

Gran had never put much faith in the local cops—except, of course, for Andy, who she loved like a son. About five years ago, she'd had her own experience with them when a string of burglaries hit local shops, including the Seabreeze Bookshop.

"They put someone in jail quick," my Gran had reported. "But they got it wrong. They didn't want to *solve* the thing. Because of course they didn't. That would be too hard. They just wanted an arrest. We tried and tried to tell them that sweet Al at the butcher's might be bad with the drink, but he had a heart of gold. But of course, Chief Lee wouldn't listen. Until the burglaries continued, and Al had an alibi as rock-solid as they come—the man was right there behind bars across the street from Chief Lee's office. Why, the chief could almost wave at Al while he had his morning coffee."

Chief Bob Lee was still in office with his philosophy of *lock them up and hope we get it right.* No, I absolutely could not give the cops that phone.

I could almost hear Anna tell me, *You look out for you.* She was cheering me on even now, just as she had urged me to be firm and decisive in my business dealings. Having run a business for as long as she had, she'd served as a kind of mentor as I learned the ropes when visiting my gran. As soft-spoken as she was, I'd seen her firmly put suppliers in their place along with any others who tried to take advantage of her caring nature. Now in the quiet of my store, I heard her ask for help. *As for the creep who did it, make sure he gets his butt kicked halfway to New Hampshire. Oh, and one more favor, Rue? Cook him in a bonfire while you're at it.*

I promise, I told her. But how could I promise that? I could match a reader to the perfect book, but that was about the limit to my skill set. A detective I was not.

As I knelt to unpack the bookplates, Elizabeth wandered over. "You know, Rue, I've been thinking," she said quietly. "The last time I saw Anna in here, things did seem kind of off." But before she could continue, we were startled by the tinkling of the bells above the door. Slowly, I looked up from my spot on the floor, and my heart sunk when I saw a man's black shoe and caught the sparkle of a badge.

CHAPTER THREE

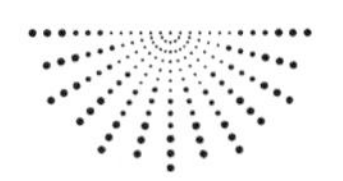

Thank Dostoyevsky it was Andy.

Quickly I stood up. "Tell me you have news."

"Well, they didn't find a weapon, which would have been convenient. A weapon, preferably with fingerprints, is what you want to find. So no real leads at this point. Just a tragic day."

"Where did they find her, Andy?" Elizabeth came toward us.

"The side entrance to the bakery. That's the one she always used to go up to her apartment. We found a bag of books." He turned to me. "So I guess you saw her yesterday."

Ah, yes. The bag of books. That put me on the radar.

He took a notebook from his jacket. "Which of you

ladies spoke to her? Did she say anything at all that you think might be of help?" The cops seemed to have pulled him in on this one, as they sometimes did.

"She left just before I closed," I said. "We didn't talk for long. She said she didn't feel good, thought she might be getting sick. She picked up some mysteries, some of the older Rachel Thornes."

He wrote in his notebook. "I guess you might have been the last to see her. So even something small she said could be important, Rue."

Elizabeth shot me a look.

I read it loud and clear. I could decipher all her looks, from *That customer's a talker* to *You're not fooling me.* This particular version of Elizabeth's raised right eyebrow had a different meaning: *Go ahead and do it. Tell Andy what you found.*

If I told anyone in town besides Elizabeth, he would be the one. Almost from the start of my days in Somerset Harbor, Andy, Elizabeth, and I had become a tight-knit little circle; the three of us just clicked. Each of us was privy to the other's secrets. Like that Andy's doctor might force him to stop working if his new blood pressure pill didn't do the trick.

And beyond his loyalty to me was the promise he'd made to my gran to keep a watchful eye on me. She'd been like a mother to him while his parents ignored their household to sit on nearly every prestigious board in town. When it had become apparent to my gran that the little neighbor boy needed some attention, she'd invite him in for snacks and help him with his homework. While the other kids did posters on Solar System Day, Andy and Gran had come up with an elaborate model of the sky with Super Balls as planets.

He'd risk a lot for Gran. But this was a big secret to ask him to keep.

Elizabeth pulled a chair up to the Book Nook so all three of us could sit. Andy leaned back in his chair; his bottom buttons strained against his ample belly. "We're pretty sure what happened," he told us. "Someone took her purse and ran. If it wasn't for the missing purse, we might be thinking something else. But we know she must have had at least a wallet, a credit card, or something since she'd just bought those books. So that's where we're focusing our efforts, looking at this thing as a likely snatch-and-run."

Elizabeth stared hard at me. This time she raised *both* eyebrows. If I didn't speak up now, the cops would keep chasing down a theory that was most likely way off track.

"You know, Andy, " Elizabeth said slowly, "you might want to look a little closer at some of her relationships that might have been problematic."

"Oh, I know what you're getting at." He leaned forward in his chair. "We are well aware of that situation. So while it *appears* to be a robbery, we'll also look at her close circle—where there seems to have been some tension."

Well, at least there's that, I thought. Anna's horrible assistant had not escaped their radar.

Sweating, Andy reached into his pocket for a handkerchief. "Yes, we know all about Anna and her sister, Renee."

What? I leaned forward, startled. "I thought the two of them were close." The bakery shared a building with a jewelry shop owned by Anna's older sister. The sisters were often seen laughing over lunch or strolling peacefully along the streets with their elderly basset hound whose name was Pumpernickel. Sometimes if she worked late making jewelry, Renee would sleep over with her sister.

"Well, strictly off the record," Andy said, "there was lots of drama there, but for now we're looking hardest at the theory she was robbed."

I breathed in hard. "Don't waste your time with that. Nobody took her purse."

He looked at me, confused. "It's the only thing that makes sense. Murdered woman, missing purse..."

"It isn't missing, Andy. Her purse is in my desk."

He leaned back in surprise then studied me intently. A moment of silence passed. "Okay, Rue, what's up?" he asked me warily.

"Just between us three?" I asked.

He closed his eyes and frowned before he seemed to make up his mind. "I hope I won't regret this. But okay, Rue, talk to me."

"Better yet, I'll show you." With my heart in my throat, I made my way into my office and took the phone out of the purse along with a piece of paper on which I'd written down the awful message. I made my way back to the Book Nook and held the phone and paper out to Andy. "I was checking to make sure that the purse was hers, and I pulled out her phone. And Andy, I have no idea what this text even means that I saw on her phone. Here. I wrote it down."

He didn't take the phone. "Just give me the paper, Rue. If we're keeping this between us, I don't want any fingerprints from the victim's phone to be traced back to me. That would be a mess."

When he finished reading, he looked stunned. "Who else was in here with her?"

"Just me. This one guy and his girlfriend came in, but Anna had left by then."

"Any idea who they were?"

I shook my head. "But they didn't seem suspicious. I don't think it was them who made her write that text."

"Oh, well. Even so, I hope that they bought something."

"They just browsed. How come?"

"Credit card receipts," he said. "If we had that to go on, we could find out who they were."

Then I remembered something. "That boy, he found the purse, and then he brought it to the counter. Who knows if he'd seen her leave the store before he came in. I mean, it wasn't like we were flooded with customers. She was the only person who left the shop before he came in. If he hears on the news that the purse was stolen and he recognizes Anna…"

"Which is one of a hundred reasons you need to make a statement—an official statement to police." Andy's voice was firm. "All of these ugly truths have a way of coming out." He sighed. "Which keeps a guy like me in business. Ugly truths about ex-husbands, soon to be ex-husbands…"

"But Andy, I just can't. You heard how bad that text sounds. I don't want to be arrested! We have to figure out what that text is all about—and who did that to Anna."

He exchanged a rueful look with Elizabeth. "*We?* Did you get your detective's license when I wasn't looking?"

"What I meant was...won't you *please* try to figure this thing out? Andy, I'm so scared."

He reached across to put a hand on my arm. "Nobody's gonna lock you up based on some vague text. But I'm not gonna lie; they'll look at you real hard if they see that phone. Still, Rue, here's the thing. If that boy decides to talk, you'll be in a world of trouble. You need to tell the cops that you have Anna's purse and you need to do it now. By this afternoon, they'll have Anna's picture all over the TV. And if the boy goes to the cops to correct the information about the missing purse..."

"You might be right," I said. "I seem to be in trouble either way."

"Oh, and by the way," said Elizabeth. "Just before you came in, I was mentioning to Rue that I've had a thought. The last time I saw Anna, she did seem kind of troubled. When I first heard about what happened, it did not occur to me to connect it with a killing. It was just a box of pictures, not at all a thing to get a person stabbed. It was really nothing. But now that I think about it, it might be *something* after all."

Andy and I talked anxiously over one another as we urged her to go on.

CHAPTER FOUR

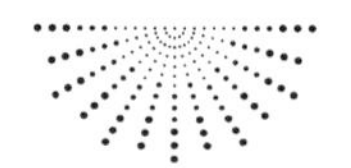

Elizabeth glanced at me, then fixed her gaze on Andy as she let out a long breath. "Lately, Anna had started spending time in my part of the store when she came in to browse. She was always very friendly, but it was only in the last few weeks that she showed any interest in my little treasures. And that was fine by me. Leftovers from the past aren't to everybody's taste. Anna's tastes ran more to mysteries, and she was always up for reading a good thriller. Oh, and anything to do with France. She was really into that."

My heart would not stop thumping. "Elizabeth, I love you, but will you please get to the point?"

"And was there a special something that she was looking for?" Andy asked.

"She said she had an interest in that old commune,"

Elizabeth said. "Do you know the one? It used to be just east of town, on that stretch of Bayhill Road that narrows to one lane."

Andy nodded. "I seem to remember that it was rather small—only several families living out there on the farm, growing their own food. They were pretty self-sufficient, hardly ever came to town. They weren't troublemakers, although they'd get irritated at the school kids who'd drive by to stare. Kids used to call them names since they were a little different. I think it was in the seventies they all up and left."

"Why did Anna care about some commune that's been gone for that many years?" I asked.

"She didn't say." Elizabeth was thinking hard. "She spent a lot of time one day with a couple of old scrapbooks I had from the sixties. And boxes of old photos. That was the day I noticed she was not herself. She seemed jumpy, out of sorts, and you know how Anna always was—they don't make them any sweeter."

"It's one thing to be jumpy but did she seem *terrified?* Like she said in the text?" I asked. "I talked to her a lot, and she seemed the same as always. Which is why that awful text just seems so mystifying."

Elizabeth shook her head. "What she seemed to be was nervous. Once, someone else walked in, and she kind of jumped and asked 'Elizabeth, who's that?' Like she wanted it to be a secret she was looking at the stuff."

Andy furrowed his brows. "Very strange."

"And once, I heard her on the phone. She had some old pictures spread out on the table, and she picked up her cell. I couldn't hear a lot of the conversation, but... oh, wait a minute." Elizabeth rushed back to her corner and came back with a red cloth notebook.

"You wrote it down, the things she said?" Andy asked.

"It's something new I started. I write down things that people say when they come in my space. Because here's what I imagine: the words all printed out in some antiquey font and strung out in a display. You know, things like *Fascinating! Thrilling! A kind of timeless beauty.* I'd put quotes around them. And that way customers would know that this was not a case of me tooting my own horn, but instead it would be a—"

"Please, Elizabeth," I interrupted. "What did Anna say?"

"Well, what I did *not* expect to hear—and what I most certainly *cannot* string up on a display—is the following." She looked down at her open notebook. *"Things I wish I hadn't seen... Just a horror show."*

"Now that you mention it," I said, "when she came in here, I saw that her hand was trembling when she handed me her credit card. I thought she'd probably overdone it on the caffeine like I do sometimes. But when I think about it now, the few times we went for coffee when I was in town, she always had decaf."

Elizabeth's eyes went to the photo of the woman with the long curls who we'd been admiring earlier that day. "She asked me twice about that picture. Where I found it, who she was. She seemed very interested."

"Do you know who it is?" Andy asked.

"It came from an estate sale that I went to last month." Elizabeth turned efficient. "I'll go through my records, see what I can find out from the company that put on the sale. Although a lot of times they don't have a clue about the people in these pictures. It's the air of mystery that people like the most."

I leaned forward. "The picture of the woman—did it come from the same sale as the things that Anna picked out and spread out on the table?"

She nodded.

"And you have no idea who Anna was talking to that day on the phone?" Andy asked.

"How I wish that I had asked."

"But that person on the other end knows exactly what it was that had her spooked," I said. "What we need to do is find that person. Do you think it was Renee?"

Andy sighed. "Well, there's a story there about her sister. All kinds of things going on with that."

Before he could elaborate, a buzz sounded from his pocket. He pulled out his phone, stared at it, and frowned. "Please excuse me, ladies." He listened intently to a message before reporting back to us. "They found something near the crime scene they think might be important. It's a little piece of paper with some blood."

I sat up straight. "What kind of paper was it? Was there any writing on it?"

"Anything that might be useful?" Elizabeth asked.

He answered with a wry grin. "Useful, I suppose, if you have a craving for Anna's lemon cake. It was a recipe they found."

He stood up to take his leave and promised to update us when he could. "Think about what I told you, Rue. If you want to talk to Chief Lee, I'll be glad to go along. But if you insist on keeping your little secret, I'll come back later for the phone and see what kind of information I can get from it. I'll bet it can tell some stories, but I'll need to have some gloves on before I put a hand on it."

As he was leaving, he glanced over his shoulder. "I don't know what's going on, so promise you'll be careful."

CHAPTER FIVE

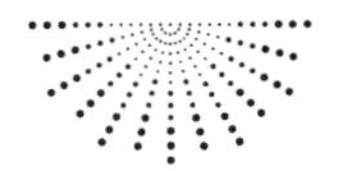

Andy almost ran into Rachel Thorne, who was coming in the door as he was going out.

"So sorry," he told her as she stepped back just in time.

Tall and magisterial, Somerset Harbor's own best-selling author was dressed in her trademark purple. The rich hues of her silky caftan seemed to make the silver in her hair shimmer even more. She wore an artsy necklace, a beautiful piece with a star-shaped pendant. "Oh, no worries," she reassured him. "I know how busy you must be. The news just makes me sick."

He nodded. "A sad day for the town."

"Any clues about what happened?"

"Working hard to find out."

She shivered as if she had only at that moment heard

about the stabbing. "We all appreciate it. I've always felt so safe here. I hope that doesn't change."

As nonchalantly as I could, I slipped Anna's phone into my pocket. "I'm so glad that you stopped by," I said to Rachel, smiling. "If you could sign more copies of *Danger After Dark*, I would absolutely love it. Those are going fast." A typical tourist sought out two things when they came into town: Anna's famous lemon cake and their very own signed copy of one of Rachel's books. Each book came with a special stamp that showed it had been purchased in the town where Rachel had written it. Her fans knew that Rachel's hometown had served as the inspiration for the backdrop in one of her most popular series.

"It would be my honor." Rachel smiled and took a silver pen out of her purse. She headed to the nearby table that was dedicated to her work. She picked up a book and frowned. "I guess you'd say that murder is my stock-in-trade. It's made me a good living, but I would just as soon it stay out of my real life and my town."

"Don't you know it," Elizabeth said. She had moved back to her corner, where she was dusting a display.

Then I heard Rachel gasp. "Where on Earth did you find *that?*" she asked. She was staring, transfixed, at the portrait of the woman with the smoky eyes.

"An estate sale I was at last week," Elizabeth said slowly as she discreetly caught my eye.

This lady with the flying pig was certainly adept at drawing strong reactions.

"Do you know who the woman is?" Elizabeth asked Rachel.

I'd never seen the famous author be anything but poised. But something that looked very much like fright flashed briefly in her eyes. Quickly she recovered. "Oh, I have no idea. It's just that she's rather...lovely, don't you think?" She paused. "Tell me, Elizabeth, were there any other items that you purchased at this sale? Maybe from the same box? I'd love to have a look. I'm thinking for my next book, I'll go back a bit in time. And you know how much your things inspire me. Stories from the past!"

"Sure. I'll put some things aside for you that came from that same sale. I think they're still in the back room. Can you come in next week?"

"If you could get to it soonish, I'll run in and take a look. You know, I'm kind of anxious. I'm in a writing mood!"

Elizabeth busied herself by opening an old scrap-book for display, draping a silk ribbon artfully across the cover. I knew what she was up to. There was nothing of Elizabeth's stored in the back room. She wanted us to be the first to have a look at these boxes, which Rachel and Anna both had zeroed in on.

Rachel signed some books and browsed a little before she headed for the door. "Oh, and by the way," she said, "I love your new addition. I think every bookstore ought to have a cat!"

I looked at her, confused.

Nuzzling at her ankles was my little furry friend.

"Oh, he's not a bookstore cat," I said, "although I have to say, he's trying awfully hard to be one."

As I reached down for the kitten, a vibration filled my pocket.

"Well, I'll let you go," Rachel said as she reached for the door. "I can see you have a call."

I was too stunned to answer. *Someone was calling Anna's phone.*

CHAPTER SIX

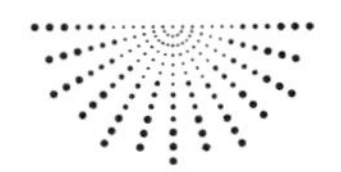

I stared down at the screen. What would happen if I answered?

The person might demand to know what the heck I was doing with their dead friend's phone.

Or they might not have heard the news. And this call could be a clue.

Elizabeth and I were alone now in the store.

I hit *Accept.* "Hello?"

Elizabeth put her hand on her hip and stared, amazed that I'd had the nerve to answer.

The woman on the other end spoke with a heavy accent. "Anna, darling! Got your message, and yes, we have to chat. This absolutely must be dealt with! And Papa? Oh, poor Papa! Papa doesn't know! Could I bear to break the news to Papa? We will tell him if we must—

but for now, let's wait and see." She sighed. "Oh, and Anna, please be careful. There is no telling now what that horrid creature might decide…" She paused, and I heard her speaking to a child before she returned to "Anna."

"Sweetie, I'm so sorry," she continued. "One of the babies always needs me; it is my lot in life that I never get to have a single conversation that lasts more than half a second. Oh! And the fleur-de-lis!" She was speaking loudly now, over the wailing of a baby. "Do not forget the fleur-de-lis!" She sighed. "We always were so sure that the fleur-de-lis would save us."

"Well, I—"

I was interrupted by the sound of something crashing.

"Oh, for heaven's sake," the caller said. "These kids! Hope no one broke an arm. Anna, I must run. Love you, love you, love you! We'll talk soon, and in the meantime, stay safe and stand your ground." With that, she was off.

"Well," Elizabeth said, "I can't say that was the smartest thing you've ever done, but I'm dying to know more."

"I have no idea what *that* was all about." I explained as best I could how the conversation—or the monologue—had gone.

We fell into a silence, both of us kind of stunned.

"Did Anna ever talk about a fleur-de-lis?" asked Elizabeth. "Or was there anything she owned with that kind of decoration?"

"Not that I remember."

"Hmm." Elizabeth reached down to pet Gatsby, who was nuzzling at her leg. "Before you got that phone call straight from Weirdsville, I was about to blame our town's esteemed author for the murder," she said with a wry smile. "Of course, you know I'm kidding, but what's up with that box from the estate sale? That stuff had Anna spooked, and Rachel zeroed right in on that picture of the woman."

"Yeah, Rachel couldn't wait to get her hands on anything else you might have gotten from that sale," I said. "Something's up with that."

"Well, what are we waiting for?" Elizabeth headed back to her corner of the shop. "Let's see what we have." She put the box up on a table that she'd set up for guests who loved to linger and peruse. "I've unpacked a few things that I bought that day, but most of what I have is still packed up in here."

I sat down in one of several chairs that were placed around the table. "Did most of the things, you think, belong to the same person? Or to just one family? How does that work exactly?"

"Every sale is different, but in this case, everything

they had for sale came from the estate of a local couple whose house is on the market." Elizabeth pulled a stack of postcards from the box. "I don't know their names. But that's something I can check."

I looked through the stack of postcards. "None of these have writing. So I guess that someone bought them to keep as souvenirs." There were cards that featured a theater in Miami, sunken gardens in Florida, and street scenes in busy cities with old-fashioned cars; there were flying birds whose greens and reds had held their brightness through the years.

Next, I picked up a sketchbook filled with landscapes and faces that could have been photographs; they were just that real. Someone had a lot of artistic talent.

"What was it that Anna had out on the table the day she got upset?" I asked.

"Oh, hang on. Let me get that stuff. I put it on that shelf behind you after she went home." Elizabeth stood up and came back with her arms loaded down. "Here are the photos she was looking at, and she also had these scrapbooks." Elizabeth began looking through a scrapbook while I went through a stack of photos.

The photos were black and white and were pretty standard stuff: family shots on the beach and around a Christmas tree; a toddler on a bike. In a couple of large group shots, I saw a girl who I thought might be a younger version of the woman in the photo that had so intrigued Anna and Rachel both. But I could not be sure.

"Now *this* is interesting." Elizabeth stared down at a brochure taped into a scrapbook. "A museum for—are you ready?—a museum for antique keys. Can you imagine such a thing? That sounds magical to me."

"And *familiar* too." I thought about it for a moment. "Where have I heard of that before?" I found another picture that I was almost sure was our mystery woman. The camera seemed to have caught her by surprise, and she was laughing. She was loading a small suitcase into a car with a dog close at her heels. "This is her." I handed Elizabeth the photo.

And that's when I remembered. "There was a key museum in Rachel's book—the first one that she wrote. *Death is Not a Stranger Here."*

Elizabeth sat back and took that in. "Do you think that Rachel's first book was about the people in these pictures?"

"It could have been," I said. "But it wasn't just that one book. She wrote her whole first series about those characters." Then a chill ran through me. "Oh, Elizabeth," I said.

She peered at me, concerned. "You're scaring me. What is it?"

"Anna had just bought those. That was the series she was reading when she died."

"And what happened to the people in the books?"

"Well, it wasn't very pretty." I hadn't read the books in years, but I explained as best as I could remember. The series was about a town in Massachusetts plagued by a series of brutal killings, ranging from a strangling in an alley to a "fall" off a high bridge that was not a fall at all.

"How did our woman fare? Or do I want to know?"

"Well, there are lots of women in the book. You know how Rachel writes. She loves a family saga, and all her books are long. There's no character I remember that jumps out as being her. Besides, the book is fiction."

Elizabeth leaned back in her chair. "Or maybe not," she said. "Could some of the really awful parts be real? Maybe that's what Anna was starting to find out."

"Oh, my gosh. That's true! Rachel could have taken real events and changed a lot of details. That's what a lot of writers do. Like did you know that Stephen King was thinking of a real hotel when he wrote *The Shining?*"

"No way! That's terrifying. Please tell me that it doesn't come complete with those creepy twins."

"Well, supposedly, ghost children *do* play out in the hall. And the maid that would clean your room? They say that one of them hasn't been alive in, well...for a long, long time."

"Okay, if any more of *his* stuff happened in real life, I don't want to know. I'll take Book One, okay? You can take Book Two of that first series Rachel wrote. We'll see what we can find that might match up to this stuff that seemed to freak Anna out."

"And to our mystery woman. She seems to be important, judging from the way that Anna and Rachel seemed almost startled by her picture."

But a part of me was wary. I was afraid my bedtime reading might leave me too afraid to sleep.

CHAPTER SEVEN

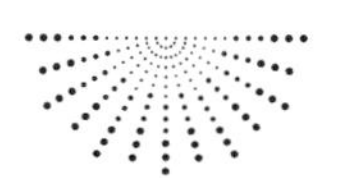

When the bell tinkled on the door, I looked up to see Carson Bentley from Bentley's Ice Cream Castle. I stood up to greet the gray-haired lanky man as he ambled through the door. Gatsby happily barked hello, meeting Carson at the entrance. My smart dog had learned by now which customers to count on for head rubs or little treats.

"Well, if it isn't Carson Bentley. *Making Ice-Cream Magic Since 1992,"* I teased. His famous little jingle could usually get a laugh.

This time, though, was different. Instead of his hearty belly laugh, he gave me a sad smile. "Oh, Rue, can you believe it? I feel like I've lost a daughter."

When his own daughter, Kate, had moved to Texas with her family the year before, it had been hard on

Carson. He missed the three small boys who'd always tagged along, eating ice cream or fishing with him on Lake Sinclair. With the grandchildren now away, Anna had stepped up. She'd invited Carson to the family seafood boils her father loved to host. She insisted that he stop in after hours to taste-test her spice cake with maple bacon glaze. On her Thursday afternoons off when I'd visited last, we'd see her lingering at the Castle, listening with a smile to the long-winded, never-ending stories that Carson loved to tell.

I gave him a sympathetic smile and moved toward him for a hug. "I know what you mean," I said. "A lot of us cherished Anna."

After we shared some of our favorite Anna stories, he glanced through the history section, and I went back to the orders that I was working on. After a few minutes, I looked up. "Hey, I'm glad that you came in, Carson." I walked toward a nearby shelf. "We've just got in a new book that's just your kind of thing. It's mostly fiction, but George Washington is in it. And Ben Franklin too—and a time-traveling professor from 1983." It was, in fact, a perfect mashup of Carson's favorite subjects.

"Oh yeah?" This time, his smile was real. "And you say you've got a copy?"

"Right here in my hand." I held it out to him.

I made us some tea as he headed to the Book Nook. Then I sat quietly beside him as he sighed in satisfaction and began to read.

I loved that about a book. It could take you to a better place when the place that you were stuck in had just cracked your heart wide open. Like Emily Dickinson's frigate, there was nothing like a rollicking adventure to take you far away—*Nor any Coursers like a Page Of prancing Poetry*. It all depended on your taste.

I'd spent some time that morning thinking of the people who'd be hurting most that day. And for each of them, I had a book in mind that I thought might bring them comfort. I felt some satisfaction that even in my grief, there was something I could do to help the people here.

I'd set aside a book on antique jewelry that I thought Renee would like. Once things settled down some, I planned to take it over with a box of tea. I could not imagine what she was going through. Anna and Renee had been a constant pair. Since neither ever married, they took meals and trips together, and it was a great delight to hear the two of them get the giggles. I loved to watch them gasp for air with tears rolling down their cheeks. If, as Andy said, there had been some trouble between the two of them, that would only add to Renee's despair.

Elizabeth came out to say hello to Carson. I handed her a cup of tea and then pointed another customer to our local interest section.

When we were alone again, Elizabeth let me know that she'd put in a call to Elegant Estates, which had sold her the artifacts we'd looked through that morning. Elegant Estates was owned by her pal Mel.

"I told them we'd had a lot of customers who really liked the stuff and that I was impressed," she said. "I said I had an interest in maybe seeing more."

It turned out that the house where the estate sale had been held was the family home of Barney and Lorna Harwood, both of whom had recently passed away. The items had all been owned by the Harwood family. According to Elizabeth, the Harwoods were once prominent in town, but their numbers had begun to dwindle in the nineties. Now there was only a single grandson, who was childless and living in Vermont.

And, as sometimes happens, the remaining heir was into modern stuff and had zero interest in heirlooms from the past.

"Even photographs?" I asked. I could understand not wanting dated couches and antique high-backed chairs with dark wood and fussy details. But selling off your ancestors in fading black and white as they picnic and wave and pose in their best suits and dresses? I asked Elizabeth who would do a thing like that.

She shrugged. "Some people just don't care. Thankfully, others do." She smiled. "And Antiquities and Curiosities by Elizabeth is right here to help with their enjoyment of fine pieces of the past. Mel says there was a lot left and that I could stop by anytime to look. You should come along."

"Yeah. We should go for sure," I said.

The bell tinkled then, and we looked up to see Andy, who was looking haggard. Elizabeth rushed to get him some of his favorite tea—green pear with a touch of sugar. "You don't look good at all," she said, handing him a cup.

"Murder investigations can tear at a man's soul. I'm getting way too old for this kind of thing," he said.

"Well, I know you need the money to do your private work, but you don't have to let the cops pull you in on their investigations too," Elizabeth told him. "You're not on *their* payroll."

He took a sip of tea. "The thing about it is, I care too much about this town to leave it up to Bob Lee to keep the bad guys off the street." He looked around the store to make sure we were alone, then he nodded his head toward me. "Plus, this one over here is asking me to keep the kind of secrets I know I shouldn't keep. That's been weighing on me too. I'm not gonna lie."

I reached out to touch his hand. "And I love you for it. I'm just in a mess."

"It goes against the things I stand for, but on the other hand, I can see Bob Lee making an arrest too fast, based only on that phone. He'd do it just to prove that he's *the man,* never mind the truth. That's how things get done around this town if the good cops we have don't pay close attention."

"That's what I'm afraid of," I told him.

"The pressure's really mounting for the chief to put someone in jail. The town's all up in arms."

The familiar knot of worry took its place deep in my belly. "Any news?" I asked.

"As a matter of fact, there is. A tip came in—a good one." He looked at me and then Elizabeth. "Now, don't get too excited yet, but keep your fingers crossed. An arrest might be forthcoming."

I gasped. Could I dare to hope? "Andy, who?" I asked.

He looked down into his mug. "Well, that part is very sad. They think it was Renee. Well, not Renee herself, but someone she hired to do it."

CHAPTER EIGHT

"No way." I leaned across the counter toward Andy. The only time I'd ever wished I had a sister was when I watched Anna interacting with Renee. I used to love to watch my friend whisper in her sister's ear before they both burst into giggles.

A dark look crossed Andy's face. "Well, there were several witnesses who had seen the sisters having what appeared to be insistent, heated conversations over the past two weeks."

"Really?"

"Uh-huh. One of them said that Anna had tears in her eyes, and once, Renee had stormed out of the bakery, which isn't like Renee."

My lips pursed as I considered that. It was true that

Renee was quiet and accommodating; she hardly ever said a word, and when she did, it was in a quiet voice that was almost apologetic.

Sitting nearby, Elizabeth perked up. "What were the arguments about?"

"No idea," Andy said. "Nobody overheard any of the conversations. They just saw the cutting looks, the tears, and all of that."

Elizabeth let out a huff. "What am I missing? They're sisters; sisters fight. I'm the youngest of four sisters; I'm lucky I'm alive. Did I ever tell you about the near miss with a hairbrush that came flying at my eye when I was six? I know you're the expert, Andy, but isn't it a stretch to be looking at Renee just because there were a few disagreements with her sister?"

"You're right. There's more," he said. "Another witness, a cleaning lady for the building, had gone outside the bakery to dump trash when she happened to glance up at the window to Anna's small apartment. That's when she saw Renee, flying from desk to dresser to side table, opening drawers and rifling through her sister's stuff. The witness reported that this was on an evening when Anna was away."

"That does sound odd," I said.

"They're questioning her now," he said, "but it seems more likely that Renee would hire a killer than to stab her sister. But that would make her guilty all the same."

"I'm sure there's an explanation," I told Andy. "*Something* must have been going on between them, but I can't imagine that..."

Horrified, I let my thoughts trail off. I was sure they had this wrong.

"It's worth checking out," Andy said, "but, yeah, I'm not convinced. On the other hand, the chief, he's all over these tips that have been coming in about Anna and her sister." He frowned. "Bob Lee is on a mission to get *someone* behind bars. The community is outraged—and everyone's afraid. They're demanding answers—fast."

Elizabeth raised an eyebrow. "Never mind if it's the *right* someone who gets locked away—as long as the cameras get a picture of Bob's old ugly mug announcing an arrest." Gatsby ambled over and settled down beside her, and she reached down to touch his neck.

"Yeah, I'm really worried he might act too fast," Andy said.

My heart was racing now. "But they need to look at other things that might have been going on. Elizabeth and I might have found a link to something. We've been going through old photographs and things that Anna had a strong reaction to right before she died. And don't forget there's Jules! I'm thinking it was *Jules,* waiting outside on that bench, who made her write that creepy message."

"You might be right, and I have no doubt they'd look hard at him as well...*if* they knew about the message."

Holy Harry Potter. Andy was exactly right. My efforts to protect myself were holding back the investigation in a major way. Was my reluctance to come forward about to get Renee arrested? "Don't let them put Renee in jail," I said. "If you see that's about to happen, Andy, let me know. And I'll step forward." It was what I had to do.

"The sooner, the better," he said. "The longer you stay quiet, Rue, the bigger hole you're gonna dig to get yourself in trouble."

He was right, of course, but was there perhaps a way to find the killer—the *real* killer—before they put me or Renee in handcuffs?

Elizabeth caught my eye; she knew me all too well. "Andy, I don't think that Rue is gonna be on board yet with the ever-sensible Plan A. We need a Plan B—and fast. Let us fill you in on what's been going on with us."

We told him about the scrapbook and the photographs. We told him about the phone call "Anna" had received.

He looked at me, aghast. *"You answered the phone?"*

"Maybe not my brightest moment. That could have backfired big time, but now we have more clues."

He sat back to think. "Clues that unfortunately point in all kinds of strange directions, none of which make sense. A fleur-de-lis, Rachel Thorne's first series, and a museum *of keys?"* He sighed. "What was it that our Anna got herself mixed up in?" He paused and looked around to make sure no customers had snuck in. Then he pulled a pair of gloves from his pocket. "Okay, Rue, I think it's time that you gave me that phone. And I really hope it will do some talking."

I got it from my desk and handed it to him. "Andy, how soon will you know what else might be on the phone? This whole situation is scaring me to death."

"I'll get on it right away." He wiped some sweat from his brow. "You're not the only one who's losing sleep with this. You know this goes against my code. But what we're after is the truth." He wrapped the phone up in a cloth and placed it in a small laptop case he carried. "I'm glad that my blood pressure check was *last* week. Or else I'd have some numbers that would give my doctor fits."

"Andy, thanks. I owe you."

He winked. "Free books for life might do it. Retirement's coming soon, I hope, and the reading hammock in the backyard will get a lot of use."

When he left, I headed to the Book Nook once again and sunk back against the cushions. I had that itchy feeling in my nose that meant the tears might start flowing any minute if I didn't think calm thoughts. *Breathe in, Rue; now breathe out.*

As I closed my eyes, I felt a tiny presence in my lap, and the smallest furry paw reached up to touch my cheek. The look in the kitten's eyes seemed to share my sorrow, then he burrowed his head into my chest, and he began to purr.

Elizabeth had moved back to her corner. "How about I pick us up some sandwiches?" she called out. "We can stay late and go through the other things from the Harwood estate."

Good idea, I thought. I was really anxious to try to find out more. And it might be a good idea to spread the stuff out after hours. Then there would be no danger of Rachel coming in and seeing that we also had an interest in the stuff. I could tell by the light outside it was almost time to close.

The knot in my stomach tightened, but the kitten burrowed closer—and that helped.

"Anything else you need for me to get while I run out for the food?" Elizabeth called out as she headed for the door.

"Cat food," I replied. "A litter box, I guess?"

She turned around, confused.

"We're officially cliché," I said. "We have a bookstore cat."

CHAPTER NINE

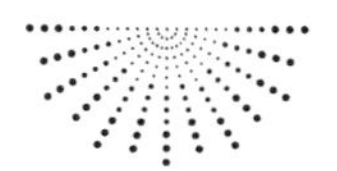

By the time Elizabeth returned with roast beef on rye, coleslaw, and a tuna-flavored feast for the newest member of the staff, I had some pictures spread out on a table in the back of the store. My goal was to arrange the photos in a kind of timeline, hoping some kind of story might emerge. The first shots seemed to date back to a day before "ML" was born. (That's what we'd begun to call her—short for Mystery Lady.) There were wedding photos of her parents, and then the young couple was shown posing with their growing family of small boys. Then finally, a baby girl appeared in frilly dresses.

Judging from the general time frame of the pictures, we guessed that Barney Harwood was one of the boys. And we figured the mystery lady was his sister—apparently, the only girl born into the family. One more boy seemed to have come shortly after ML to complete the large and boisterous family. According to my timeline of photographs, two more boys came after her till the family picture was complete.

"What are you doing?" I asked Elizabeth as she stared down at her laptop. "I'm on ReadWithUs.com," she said. "If we think there's a chance they're about to arrest Renee, I don't think you and I have time to sit down and read Rachel's books. Or reread, in your case. So I'm skimming some reviews to see if there are things that I should look for in these pictures."

"Good idea," I said, watching as the kitten batted at the fringes of a tablecloth beneath one of Elizabeth's displays. Then he ran to his now-empty bowl and gave the most pitiful little cry that I think I've ever heard.

Elizabeth looked at him at frowned. "Dramatic much?" she said. "He sounds like he hasn't eaten in a week—as opposed to having gobbled down a bowl full of the stuff within the last ten minutes."

Once again, the kitten cried, moving closer to his bowl, and a phrase from Charles Dickens popped into my mind. *Please, sir, I want some more.*

"Oh, Oliver Twist," I cooed, "you've already had your dinner. We'll call him Oliver! They're both such charming little orphans."

Elizabeth rolled her eyes. Then Oliver ran up to her and rubbed his head against her leg. The next thing that I knew, she was spooning food into his bowl. "Just a little extra," she explained to me. "It's his first day in a new home. That calls for dessert."

The kitten soon fell asleep cuddled next to Gatsby as I continued to place the pictures chronologically. After about twenty minutes, I became concerned. In the latest family group shots, with grandchildren now included, our gorgeous Miss ML was nowhere to be seen. The brothers in the meantime had progressed into middle age with more fat around their bellies and less hair on their heads.

"Elizabeth, come look at this," I said, explaining my concern about our lady's absence from the pictures. "People back in those days tended to stay close to home. So where did ML go? You don't think that..." I didn't like to think of all the murders in the books that might —or might not—be partially about this family.

We studied the last photos of her, several of which included a tall, handsome man with a head full of dark curls. On the beach or in front of a huge old-fashioned car, he held her hand in his or kept his arm protectively around her.

I sighed. "Isn't that her luck? She seems to have just *vanished*—and it had to happen while she's going out with absolutely the most gorgeous man who ever walked the earth. Would you *look* at that man's eyes?"

Elizabeth's eyes went wide. "Oh, dear. This isn't good at all."

"What do you mean?" I asked.

"I've been reading the reviews of *Death is Not a Stranger Here* while you've been doing this. And a young woman in the book drowns in Lake Sinclair—the same year she gets engaged."

"Oh, that's right," I said, dismayed. "I remember—kind of. Although it's been so long since I read the book." I studied the last pictures of our lady. In one, she gazed up at the man with a look of adoration. And he looked back at her as if he wished the person with the camera would go away already so he could lean down with a kiss.

"And the woman in the book, or at least the way she's written, seems to be quite the witch," Elizabeth continued. "This character—Clarinda—is written as a snob. She's supposedly this diva who tells her brothers and everyone around her what to do. And, worst of all, she seems to have stolen her fiancé from her former best friend." She sighed. "These reviews give you so much detail, why bother with the books?"

In another picture, ML was looking at the camera as

if she and the person on the other end shared some inside joke they both found delightful.

"I'm almost as good at reading people as I am at reading books," I said. "And I think we'd like this woman. I think we'd want this woman to go to the movies with us and to be our new best friend. I don't think she was a diva. I'm pretty sure she kept it real."

"Well, as you said, it's just a book. Rachel might have started out with someone real in mind but then made up a lot of stuff." She picked up a photograph. "But I think we're on to something. This character—Clarinda—was the only girl in a family of five brothers. And in the book, her 'drowning' turned out to be a murder by a neighbor."

"Why did he kill our lady?" I sank down in my chair.

"Not our lady! He killed *a character.* You have to remember, Rue, that this is just a book! But according to the website that I looked at, the neighbor was avenging all kinds of stuff, it seems. Stuff to do with money, love...the usual kinds of drama that you find in these kinds of sagas."

"Well, it may be a made-up story, but Rachel for some reason is really, really anxious to get her hands on these things."

"And when Anna took an interest, when she started asking questions—someone stabbed her to death."

"It could be there's too much truth in whatever Rachel wrote." I paused to think about my next step. "Rachel asked about that commune. Was there a commune in the book?"

"There could have been, I guess. But I haven't seen it mentioned so far in the reviews." Elizabeth stared down at the table, her hands on her hips. That always meant some kind of plan was brewing in her mind. "Tomorrow, Rue," she said, "I'll try to see if Mel will give me some contact information for the grandson who was selling all this stuff. I'll say I have a client with an interest in that period who is on the hunt for some specific things...things related to the commune and related to..." She paused to gaze down at the picture. "And related to female artists from the late sixties...early seventies here in Massachusetts. Perhaps that will get the grandson to talk about his great aunt. Because I guess that's what she was."

I looked down at the photo and saw that our lady had on a sweatshirt that read *Creekside Institute of Art.* She must have been the one who'd filled the sketchbook with such elaborate and realistic looking scenes and faces.

Elizabeth nodded to herself. "I say we pack this stuff up and keep it at my house. It seems to have drawn a lot of interest. If we aren't super careful, I wouldn't be surprised if it up and disappeared while we were closed."

"You might be right," I said. As we began to pack up, I glanced out the window to see a figure on the bench, sitting very still by himself in the dark. *Jules.*

Elizabeth looked as well when she heard me gasp. "How creepy is that, Rue? Everything is closed now. What is he even doing?"

"I'll call Andy right away," I said. *Breathe in,* I thought. *Breathe out.* "He'll make sure we get out safely."

CHAPTER TEN

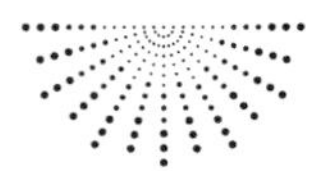

Andy and I followed Elizabeth home, then he pulled in behind me in my driveway.

"I have some Jameson," I said. "I know that it's your favorite. A glass of whiskey for your trouble?"

"Don't mind if I do." Slowly, he heaved himself out of his blue Camry. "Today has been exhausting."

We sat out on the front porch with our drinks, enjoying the cool breeze that smelled of the sea. Andy was too tired to notice that there was a kitten with us in addition to the usual sleeping dog.

"Any luck with Anna's phone?" I asked.

"No time. Things just got too busy. The case took…I guess you'd say a wild turn…after Renee was questioned." He paused. "Are you ready, Rue? Here's where it gets crazy."

"I was thinking we'd passed crazy a *long, long* time ago."

My sarcasm went unnoticed as Andy sipped his drink. "I guess you're like all the others—a fan of Anna's lemon cake?" he asked.

I remembered the bloody recipe they'd found on the scene. "They think *that's* why someone killed her? That it was all because of *cake?*" Anna's lemon cake was famous, having been written up in several travel magazines, complete with full-color pictures. The chamber of commerce loved it. Every story came with information about what to do (and buy) in our little town in addition to indulging in a scrumptious taste sensation.

"Well, apparently that recipe was causing quite a stir." He winced. "And the awful pun was absolutely not intended." He rubbed at his forehead. "I'm way too tired for puns. Anyway, Renee told us she'd been looking for the recipe when she was spotted in the window. Anna had apparently been getting lots of pressure to share her ingredients, some of which were secret."

"And the cops think that's a motive to stab someone to death?" I took a sip of whiskey. The recipe, I guessed, might be worth a pretty penny. But enough to kill? People were lined up down the block outside of Anna's when the season was at its height, and I knew she shipped out a lot of cakes, on holidays especially.

"People have been killed for a whole lot less than that," Andy said. "Of course, I thought that anything that our Anna ever made was just to die for." He closed his eyes. "Pun not intended once again. But all I know is that Renee had little information about who was after Anna for the recipe. She did, however, say that Anna had been out of sorts for the past few weeks."

"Really?"

"Yeah, and it had taken Renee a while to get her sister to open up about the reason why. Seems like requests to get the recipe were really nothing new, but this time things were different."

"Different how?"

Andy pursed his lips. "Well, Renee said that Anna's hands were shaking during the one time they briefly talked about it."

"Why would she not tell her sister who it was?"

"Anna said she wanted to handle it herself and that she 'had a plan,' whatever that might mean. And now Renee is sick with guilt that she didn't just step in and ask her sister what was up. She thinks that Anna wanted to protect her, that if she said too much, Renee would be in danger too. Which she might well have been."

"Over *a recipe for lemon cake?* Andy, this is nuts."

"Killers can be crazy. Crazy's never a good reason not to chase down a lead. Anna asked Renee if the recipe was locked up in a safe. And Anna told her sister that she had no idea. She knew the recipe by heart. It had been forever since she'd seen it written down." Then, two days before the murder, when Anna was away, Renee had set out to make sure there was no copy of the recipe anywhere in Anna's place. Because she felt that recipe could get her sister killed."

"And they believed her story, right?"

Andy sighed. "Well, I, for one, think she's being truthful. It's one of my superpowers. I can tell whose tears are genuine and who's lying through their teeth to save their sorry butts. But as for Chief Lee and the others, Renee's not off the hook. Still, they're looking really hard at this new angle with the cake."

I thought about it as I rocked and took a slow sip of whiskey. "The cops found that bloody copy of the recipe *after* Anna died," I said. "And it was two days *before* the murder that Renee was looking for it. Did she say she found it?"

"She says that she did not."

"Why was it lying on the street after Anna died?" We sat in the quiet for a moment. "And there's still that creepy Jules," I said. "Why is he always *watching* out there in the dark?"

"He's on Chief Lee's list as well. Supposedly, tensions between Jules and Anna were at an all-time high."

"Plus, I'm even more convinced there's something up with Rachel Thorne."

"What about her?"

"For starters, the mystery woman I'd seen in those family photos was no longer in them, at one point. Like she just disappeared."

Andy kept his gaze fixed on me, as if he was urging me to go on.

I continued, "I might be going out on a limb here, but the disappearance seems to mirror one of the literary murders that made Rachel famous. Which might explain why Rachel almost had a fit when she saw the woman's picture in the store. What if she knows some things about a murder in the real world that she doesn't want to say?"

That earned me "the look" as he stood up to go. "Those are only *some* of those family's photos," he reminded me. "The lovely bride herself most likely kept the later ones—in which she lived happily ever after, I can almost bet, with her husband and five children and two dogs." A dark look passed over Andy's face. "Oh, and Rue, there's something else that came up in the statement they took from Renee."

The familiar knot grabbed hold of my stomach as I waited.

"Renee says that there was this one night about a

week ago that Anna called her, all upset. Anna seemed almost sure that someone was out to hurt her and that they were somewhere really close. The chief investigator asked Renee what it was that Anna had been doing right before she called. Where had Anna gone that night, who had Anna seen?" Andy looked uncomfortable.

"Andy, what did she say?" The knot in my stomach tightened even more.

"Rue, she'd been to the bookstore the night she was so upset. That made the chief take notice. So just a little bit of a heads up. They might have some questions for you. I wouldn't be surprised if they came in tomorrow."

Unable to get out any words, I sunk back down into my chair, glad at least there was more whiskey. Why had there been *two* occasions in my store when Anna had been frightened? I could not wrap my head around what might be going on.

CHAPTER ELEVEN

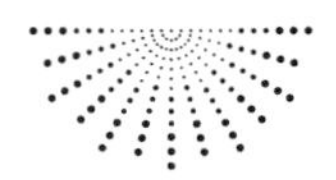

The next morning, I was running on very little sleep. The night before had passed with fitful dreams of flashing lights in blinding blue and lots of wailing sirens. I'd startled awake at least three times. My heart was still pounding hard against my chest, even without my usual two cups of morning coffee.

I'd told Elizabeth about Andy's updates—and about the official visitors who might be popping in. Every time the bell jingled on the door, I flinched, thinking it might be the cops.

When the store was quiet, Elizabeth handed me a paperback. "For your reading pleasure," she told me with a wink.

I looked down at the cover: *Spell Her Name in Blood* by Rachel Thorne.

"It's the sequel," Elizabeth said. "Of course, there's no Mystery Lady, but some of the characters are the same as the ones in the first book, and one of them is the killer. You told me Anna picked up several in the series on the night she died."

"Yeah, I think that she bought three. And she could have been looking through them in the store when she wrote that note. These might have been the books that scared her." That was my best guess at least, that it was something in a book that had caused Anna to react and type out that text message to...whoever. And to call her sister on another night and say that she was scared. What else had Anna looked at? I paced the store and thought about it. I passed the travel section, which gave me an idea.

France. It had been her obsession. She had loved to read about French art, French recipes, French history, and anything and everything that had to do with France. She'd told me that in her twenties, she'd lived there for a year right after college—the best year of her life! She'd worked at a fine restaurant and soaked in all the culture before settling into her real life here in Massachusetts.

I browsed the titles on the shelves, wondering which book she might have chosen to pick up. She'd stopped by this section of the store almost anytime that she came in to browse. On one bottom shelf, a large book was out of place, as if someone had picked it up and put it back in a hurry. I studied the cover with its colorful depiction of a street scene in the rain. A man was holding an umbrella over a lady in an evening gown as she enjoyed a piece of cake. *All the Charms of Paris* was the title.

Hardly terrifying, I thought as I flipped through the pages, half hoping something would fall out—a note, a piece of mail. I turned to the index, thinking of the odd clues that we had so far.

I looked up *fleur-de-lis* and found a picture of a coffee shop called Francine's Fleur-de-lis. There was the slightest smudge at the bottom of the page as though someone had opened up the book to this very spot and lingered for a while. The picture was dated 1982, so Anna could have been there, I supposed. But there must be a million places in the city with that magic word somewhere in their names—or who made use of the symbol.

The bell tingled and my heart stopped. If the cops were gonna come, I wish they'd just go ahead and get it over with. But it was only Isabella from the Sailor's Delight Café, which was down the block. She gave me a little wave. "Just picking out a romance to get my weekly fix!"

"Let me know if you need some help," Elizabeth said

with a smile. "I've read a lot of those. If I want romance these days, I have to buy a book."

"I understand," Isabella replied with her trademark tinkling laugh. "But perhaps that's for the best. If the guy turns out to be a cad, you can close the book. And poof, you're done with him."

Still trying hard to calm my nerves, I looked up *lemon cake,* and surprisingly enough, I got a hit. I turned to page twenty-two and stared down at the headline. *Want the Luck of Ancient Royals? Taste This Luscious Lemon Cake. But Shhh! The Recipe's Top Secret.* I took the book over to the Book Nook and sunk down to read.

According to the story, the recipe was developed for the Marchand family in the early nineteen hundreds for the wedding of their daughter, Antoinette. Antoinette's mother, Bernadette, was descended from a royal line, and the family had long been in the upper echelon of French society. Wanting nothing but the best for the only daughter, they convinced an elite chef to come out of retirement to develop a special recipe for the wedding cake in the bride's favorite flavor.

Light and moist with Bavarian crème and a little something extra that even the connoisseurs in the elite crowd could not identify, the cake was the talk of the reception. The dessert almost eclipsed the bride herself in her designer gown and diamond-encrusted tiara, which was said to have royal provenance.

In later years, the recipe became the stuff of legend. Bernadette Marchand wanted it to be kept top secret, served at only Marchand weddings and those of select aristocratic friends. It was said that any bride or groom who took a bite of the Marchand lemon cake on their wedding day would be blessed with happiness and fortune. Several chefs throughout the years have claimed to have the recipe, but the Marchand family spokesmen have always claimed the fakes were too tart, too sweet, too dry. The family did confirm, however, that the real thing was served at the wedding of Adrienne Calloway and Dexter Lyman, the Academy-Award-winning co-stars of a host of films, including *Under a Glitter Moon.* There were pictures of Adrienne Calloway and Antoinette Marchand, both in their wedding gowns.

Then a thought hit me. Had Anna had *the* recipe? She was far from royal, having been raised right here in town, where her dad had sold insurance and her mom taught school. Or did someone *think* she had it? And was it somewhere now in the police headquarters, written on a piece of paper that was stained with Anna's blood?

My thoughts were interrupted by a deep voice. "You haven't looked up for five minutes. That must be some book."

"Oh, I'm sorry! Can I help you? Thank you for stopping in at the Seabreeze Bookshop. Today is Half-Price Wednesday on all—"

I was answered with a chuckle that didn't sound as friendly as a chuckle should. "Well, all I have is questions, and the last time that I checked, there was no charge on that. Although I might have a look around a little later if you have some books on fishing."

I recognized that voice. I stood, held my hand out, and met his steely gaze. "Please have a seat, Chief Lee. Can I get you any tea?"

CHAPTER TWELVE

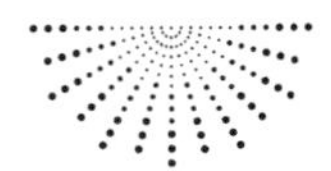

I didn't mind the questions: How had Anna seemed that night? What was on her mind? Those were questions I could answer.

What I really minded was the look that Chief Lee gave me as he stared me down. In my small back office, he leaned forward in his chair and watched me carefully, as if I were some "troublesome newcomer," as he liked to call us, with something big to hide.

And—ouch, this was the hard part—I supposed the chief was right. Oh, not that I was troublesome! That was just not me. But I *was* hiding something—that could soon explode. I took a deep breath and exhaled. *Calm down, Rue. You've got this,* I said to myself. I took comfort in the knowledge that I was on the side of good. I was keeping secrets—but in service of a higher kind of truth.

After all, I told myself, if Chief Lee saw that phone, he'd go after me, no doubt. And I wanted him to focus all of his resources on the jerk who murdered Anna.

My inquisitor towered over me with a stern expression that seemed to suck all of the life right out of the store. Then he ran a hand over his balding head. "Well, you know where to find us, Rue, if you think of something else. I want this person off the street—and soon." He crossed his arms and glared as if he were mad at *me* and not the person with the knife. In his head, I imagined, he was cursing the "outsiders" and the mayhem they brought with them to his peaceful town.

Gatsby lay at my feet in a watchful pose, growling softly at the chief. My faithful furry buddy could always sense a bad vibe, although they were few and far between at the Seabreeze Bookshop.

I shifted in my seat. "Did you know Jules Granger kind of hangs around at night?" I asked. "He's always on that bench between my place and the bakery. I always thought it was so weird, the way that he just *sits* out there in the dark when all the stores are closed." I cocked my head at the chief. "Something makes me wonder if Jules was out there waiting on that night when Anna left the store."

He waved away the tip as if it were so much rubbish. "Jules is an okay guy, Rue. A little odd, not exactly one of us. But as far as we can tell, the guy is fine. He didn't have an alibi. But that happens more than not with guys who live alone."

"He made things hard on Anna. Here, she gave him work, and he seemed to go head to head with her on every little thing."

"Yeah, we've heard about the trouble between the two of them. But that's hardly motive for the guy to up and stab his boss. There are other ways than knives to fix an employment situation that's gone bad. It's called *Get another job.* And from what I understand, he already had his bags packed by the time this thing went down with Anna."

Startled, I set down the bookmark I'd been twirling in an attempt to calm my nerves. Packing up his bags and making plans to disappear? I was no detective, but did that not scream *suspicious*?

"What kind of job?" I asked. "And where is it that he's going?"

The chief looked startled by the question. "Now, that I didn't ask."

Was it any wonder that the little bit of crime we had in our town mostly went unsolved? I made up my mind to figure out exactly what was up with Jules.

As the chief walked out of my office, Oliver rushed up to him and nuzzled at his ankle.

He looked down and smiled. "Well, isn't that a cute one? New member of the staff?"

"Yeah, he just showed up one day with that little face —how could we say no?"

Once the chief was gone, I looked down at the kitten. "Well, look at you, you little charmer. I didn't think that anyone could ever charm Bob Lee."

Oliver responded by pouncing at the bow on the pair of pricey low heels I'd bought the week before.

"No, you don't," I told him as I moved my foot away.

Turning my attention to the store, I glanced toward the counter. Elizabeth was wrapping a book in birthday paper for Katie Lyman, who sold olive oil and gourmet cheeses in a shop across the street.

"Katie, I hope your mom enjoys that cookbook." Elizabeth handed her the package. "Oh, and be sure to try the apple fritters on page fifty-four. Nothing less than little bits of heaven all fried up into balls! Top those things with sugar, and don't forget to call me when you do!"

"That sounds amazing," Katie said.

I joined them at the counter to catch up on Katie's life and recommend a new historical romance that I thought she'd like. She bought that one too.

Once she was out the door, I glanced toward Elizabeth, wondering if she had overheard the news the chief had given me on Jules.

As other customers browsed peacefully nearby, she said in a low voice, "You know what I want for lunch? A big old piece of Black Forest cake from Anna's—and I need a latte! Hazelnut, I think. I had salmon yesterday with just a little bit of salad. You can't eat healthy all the time; you have to live a little."

Oh, yes. I imagined that she had heard the news. And that she was just like me—very, very anxious to see what was up with Jules.

When my part-timer, Ellen, came in that afternoon, I told Elizabeth to get her bag. "My stomach's growling at me," I said. "Ellen, would you like for us to bring you anything from the bakery?"

"Oh, I would love to have some lemon cake. I dream about that cake sometimes." On the topic of sweets, she was a bit more talkative than usual. Then she thought again. "But I think I'll save that treat for another day when I'm in town with the kids. Thank you anyway." She was a young mother who worked a few hours every day while her children were in school. A big fan of mysteries, I think she did it more for the employee discount than the check.

At the bakery, things seemed somber, despite the colorful array of sweets underneath the counter. The tantalizing smells wafted through the cold air; the air conditioner in the place was always turned up high.

The tables, as usual, were filled, and the line to order was almost out the door. But the usual laughter and loud voices had been replaced that day with somber talk.

I nodded at Jane Castleton, a grandmotherly, friendly woman who'd been serving up cakes at Anna's since the store's first week in business. She gave me a sad smile.

When it was almost our time to order, I reached out to squeeze her hand. She held on for a little while, acknowledging our loss. Then she reached into the case to fill the orders of the customers that were ahead of us.

There was a kind of shtick I always did with Anna. And now Jane, her voice gone soft, jumped in with Anna's lines.

"Ah, the literary ladies, who are smart enough to know that every book is better with a piece of cake."

"And every slice of cake tastes better with a book," I said, as I always did to Anna. I felt the tears threatening to well up in my eyes. "Oh, Jane, I'd ask you how you're doing, but I already know the answer. I just can't believe that Anna's gone."

Elizabeth cocked her head. "How is Renee?" she asked.

"Not so good," Jane said. She handed the slices of

lemon cake to the two tall women waiting in front of us. The women paid and moved to a table.

"You know that Renee was going through so much already," Jane continued with a sigh. "The poor woman's life was in a shambles even before we lost our Anna. And the only time I ever saw Renee with a smile on her face in these past few weeks was when she was with her sister."

"I hadn't heard," I said. "What's up with Renee?"

Jane winced. "I guess I'm speaking out of turn. Renee's a private person, doesn't advertise her business. So do me a favor, Rue, and forget me and my big mouth. But, hey, if you see Renee, she might appreciate—"

Jules swept up to the counter, interrupting us. "What can we get you, ladies? May I suggest the orange cream chiffon? It's our newest cake. An inspired suggestion for the menu from me, myself, and I. And I must say it's divine." What he was saying—without saying—was *no chit-chat, move along.*

We found a great table by the window and settled in on the cushiony, comfy chairs. I took extra-big bites of my Key lime pound cake and stuck my fork more than once into the chocolatey cherry goodness that called to me from Elizabeth's plate. It was as if a part of Anna were still here to soothe us with her special brand of comfort.

Jules moved through the room with a king-like air, keeping an eye out for something to correct: a piece of cake sliced too thick or too thin, a foam heart outlined imperfectly on a latte. At one point, his cell phone rang, and he moved to the counter to speak anxiously to the caller. *Very interesting,* I thought. I'd seen him harshly reprimand employees for doing the same thing. Cell phones were a no-no during business hours.

"I want to find out where he's moving to—and why," I mouthed to Elizabeth.

But before I could get up, I heard him mutter, "Call you back," then pocket his cell phone.

Jules continued on his rounds, then he stopped by our table. "Ladies, I must say that I'm sorry for your loss," he told us in a low voice. "I know you were close to Anna."

"And the same to you,' I said. It only seemed polite.

He glanced at my plate. "Don't you adore the cake?" he asked. "I believe it hits the perfect notes. Rich and buttery. A glaze that's bright with hints of citrus. Flavor that is bold! But not too overwhelming."

I nodded, my mouth full, before he moved on to another table with the air of a celebrity who had only so much time for each adoring fan.

Elizabeth made a face. "What is he, a sommelier?" she

asked in a low voice. "Can you get any more pretentious *about a piece of cake?*"

I rolled my eyes and gave her a little smile. "Hey, I'm really anxious to check out some more things at that house. You know the one I mean—where you found all the pictures. So how soon can we go?"

"Oh, I meant to tell you. Mel said he'd be working there on and off all week. He said we could text him and to stop by anytime."

"Cool." I stuck my fork into my cake. "You know, I'm really worried now about Renee." Anna's sister was the quieter and shyer of the two, but she had been one of the first to make sure I felt welcome when I moved to town.

I was chewing my last bite slowly when I noticed Jules talking on the phone across the street in front of the butcher shop. He looked agitated.

I looked at Elizabeth. She nodded and stood up. We were thinking the same thing.

"I think I need a little *shade,"* she said with a wink.

We moved together toward the door.

Because here is what we knew: if you stood underneath the big tree just outside the bakery, you stayed fairly hidden by its sweeping branches. Which could be entertaining—or informative—depending on the scene that might be going on around you. Conversations from the sidewalks nearby carried *very well.* If you stood there at the right time, you might just get an earful.

And so we took our places. I pretended to rifle through my purse for some lost item as we kept our ears wide open. The call was almost over, but we could hear Jules's side of the conversation loud and clear.

Periodically, he looked around to see if anyone was close, but the sidewalk next to him was empty. "But my credentials are impeccable. Beyond impeccable," he said in a low voice that could nevertheless be heard. "I will *not* be disrespected…I absolutely have a plan. And I promise the finances will fall right into place—like egg whites into butter; you have my word on that. There are things I can't reveal yet that would absolutely prove I will more than have the money."

Elizabeth stared at me with wide eyes.

We heard Jules clear his throat. "Can we *please* talk face to face?" he asked the person on the other end. "There are just a few things I must see to at my place of employment. Then I'll be right there. Don't leave!"

Elizabeth shot me a thumbs-up. "I'll follow that man," she whispered.

"I'll go with you if I can." I pulled out my phone. "I'll bet you anything that Ellen will stay longer. Her kids are all in camp this week; I think she's at loose ends."

I got the go-ahead from Ellen, and adrenaline surged

through me. I looked around and quickly spotted Jules's black SUV parked across the street. Luckily, an empty space was waiting not too far from where it sat.

"I'll go get my car and move it into place," I said. "Operation Cake Snob can commence!"

CHAPTER THIRTEEN

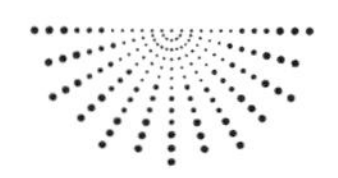

We merged onto a busy road, and I tried to keep the SUV in sight while not following too closely. With one or two cars in between us, I figured Jules could not look back and see that it was us.

Of course, said Elizabeth, it didn't really matter. "It's not all that hard to hide from someone as self-absorbed as Jules," she said. "All he ever sees is his stupid self."

After about a half hour's drive, we arrived in Hampstead, an upscale seaside town known for attracting the glitterati, who built their mansions near the water and frequented the ultra-charming little shops and cafés.

Elizabeth glanced around. "Well, ooh lah lah."

Jules pulled into a spot beside a fountain with a statue of a mermaid. The spot was clearly marked as "handicapped," but that didn't stop Jules from springing out of his SUV and striding purposefully toward his destination.

As for us law-abiding types, we drove twice around the square with not an empty space in sight.

"Did we come all this way for nothing?" Elizabeth asked.

A knot of frustration filled my chest. *Hemingway's six-toed cats!* I was determined I would somehow make this little mission work.

As I turned a corner, we spotted Jules again, walking at a quick sprint, a determined and unhappy look plastered on his face.

I slowed to a stop. "Get out," I told Elizabeth. "Find out where he's going, but don't follow him too closely. I'll text you when I park."

She got out without a word.

Eleven minutes—and three very congested blocks later—I sent her a text. *Victory at last. I think I somehow managed to get the last parking spot in all of Hampstead.*

She texted the address of a coffee shop. *It's right across from where he went. I ordered you the coffee of the day and a peanut butter brownie.*

I was glad I didn't solve crimes for a living. I would gain a hundred pounds.

A little later, we watched the crowd outside the

window as well-heeled full-time residents mixed in with eager tourists. Elizabeth explained that Jules had gone into the two-story brick building across the street.

"Gorgeous building!" I told her. The trim around the doors and windows provided charming details from an era long gone by. But I was focused on the sign in tasteful black in the top right corner of a window. *Building for Sale or Rent.*

"So, he's not running *too* far." I bit into my brownie. "What do you think he plans to do if he gets the space?"

Elizabeth picked up her latte. "I have no idea. I'm surprised he has the money to afford a Hampstead rent. But, based on what we heard, I guess he doesn't after all. Perhaps he thinks that he can just move in based on his *reputation. Impeccable,* he said. I died when he said that."

"Yeah. It doesn't work that way. Reputation is a good thing, but you need something else—ka-ching—to get approval as a renter."

From what Anna had told my gran, Jules had come to her with a résumé of low-level jobs, including work as a teaching assistant and a fry cook. Or, as he had put it on his résumé, *instructional professional* and *sous chef.* He didn't have a lot of money and rented a small apartment outside town. Nothing about the man said money.

It was partly out of kindness that Anna had taken him in as her assistant. When she'd put out the word that she was making the new hire, she had her choice of applicants. The bakery was well known throughout Massachusetts. Plus, people from Somerset Harbor all knew she'd be the perfect boss, and there was a rush of applications from the local area as well. But she'd seen a neediness in Jules as well as a shared love for fine ingredients and the way they could come together into something new.

All too soon, however, she had learned the truth. She'd mistaken greed for passion. He was not about the wonders of culinary magic. He'd been after the career boost that would come with listing Anna's Sweet Dreams Bakery on his résumé. And much like he'd given himself new titles on his application, he promoted himself quickly once he started work—although the new responsibilities, of course, were only in his mind. In truth, he was an assistant, not the man in charge, but he loved to play the part of everybody's boss.

I took out one of the small leather notebooks that we sold in sets next to the register. I jotted down some questions that I was very eager to discuss with Andy. If for some reason, Jules had expectations for a windfall, that might very well be connected to a motive. Had there been money missing from the bakery, perhaps siphoned off from the bank deposits, which Anna very often trusted Jules to make? (While working with him gave her fits, maybe she never thought he'd go so low as to steal.)

As I put an exclamation point at the end of my theory, Elizabeth touched my hand and nodded toward the scene across the street. Jules was emerging from the building, followed by a woman. His companion was a small blonde with a head full of long curls. His reddened face and expressive gestures contrasted with her stillness as they stood outside the building. She had a look on her face that mirrored the emotions that I often felt when I looked at Jules.

I eyed the woman intently. She reminded me of a real estate agent whose picture I'd seen on "For Sale" signs around town. Could that be the same woman?

"You know," I said to Elizabeth, "we should spend more time in Hampstead. It's such a lovely place and really not that far. The funeral's tomorrow. But the next day is my day to take off from work early. Why don't we come back for dinner? Maybe find a seafood place with a nice view of the water."

The idea made her smile. "And dine among the up and coming? I can do some research on some places. You know, it's really crazy, but I have not been here in years. I hear some of the newer restaurants are not to be believed."

She gazed back out the window. Jules had not stopped talking. His arms had not stopped moving.

Elizabeth pointed at me with her fork. "Dinner will be lovely. But I know you too well. I think there's more on your mind than an excellent shrimp scampi or a nice filet."

"Well." I picked up my brownie. "I thought we might stop in at the office of a certain realtor. What would you think of that? To ask about the rental of a certain *very* charming and historic place." I imagined that the agent's name was on that little sign. We could ask her how much interest the listing had so far. What kind of applicants? What plans did they have? If we were very lucky, she might feel like unloading about a certain pesky applicant with big dreams and no capital to fund them. I still had the business cards from my old career in real estate, and I could pretend that my interest in the property was professional. One professional might well be inclined to vent to another after an exasperating bout with a would-be client.

Once Jules and the agent walked away, Elizabeth and I ordered two more coffees. We wanted to make sure that Jules was good and gone by the time we stepped out onto the sidewalk. Then we wandered across the street, and I wrote the agent's name and number in my little leather book.

As I drove back to Somerset Harbor, fighting traffic now, I mused out loud to my friend. What if Jules had been stealing from the business and Anna had found out? How far might the guy have gone to make sure she didn't tell?

"I wouldn't put it past him to take money from the bakery," Elizabeth said. "But what I heard him saying was that he would have the money *in the future.*"

So what was the guy up to? I punched in Andy's number, hoping I could catch him to see what he thought.

He picked up right away. "Greetings, Rue! What's going on?" His voice rang out through the speaker.

"We've been to Hampstead sleuthing," Elizabeth put in. "A fancy place to sleuth!"

We gave him a quick update.

Andy, as it turned out, hadn't known the bit about Jules leaving town.

He let out a sigh. "I guess he told that to the chief, who didn't see the need to pass on that information to the team. That little tidbit right there could be a major piece of evidence. What was Bob Lee thinking? It's hard to investigate a murder when you don't have all the facts."

"The chief didn't seem to think it was important," I told him as I braked for a light.

"Which illustrates the reasons that whole office is a mess. But thank goodness that I have the two of you to keep me in the loop."

"So any weirdness that you've seen with the finances at the bakery?" I asked.

"None that showed up right away. But given what you've told me, I think it's worth a closer look. Crooks can be really good at hiding things. In some of the cases that I work, they only take a little bit of money at a time —amounts no one would notice." He sighed. "Sometimes it's not necessity but *greed* that's the mother of invention."

"Oh and by the way," I said, "was Renee having any problems before her sister died, something in her life that was making her upset? Did that come up when you questioned her?"

"Well, some of her employees saw her crying in the corner of her store over the last few months. And they said it happened on more than one occasion. Plus, there *were* those reports about her fighting with her sister. But Renee tells us things were fine. If there was something wrong, the woman isn't saying. Which is worrisome. As I said, Renee isn't in the clear as far as the chief's concerned. But they're not focusing on her now. They're looking more into that recipe that someone seemed to want so badly."

I thought about the story in the book, about the cake of ancient royals. But that would be too crazy, right? I was suddenly exhausted. There were so many odd paths that *might* lead to a killer with no way to pin them down. I wanted to curl up with a good book, to feel the delicious comfort of diving into drama that wasn't real at all, that belonged only in the pages. Drama that could never end with me in major trouble related to a murder. My heart rate sped up. And as dark scenarios played out in my mind, I almost ran my car into a silver Cadillac.

"Mind on the road!" said Elizabeth as her hand flew to her chest.

"Have you had a chance to work on Anna's phone and see what you can find?" I asked Andy, anxious.

Andy paused and sighed. "I do have news in that regard."

I didn't like his tone.

Breathe in, breathe out, I thought. "Okay, Andy, spill."

CHAPTER FOURTEEN

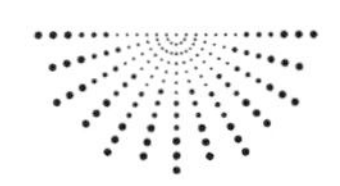

As we drove along, Andy spilled more details regarding the victim. Anna, it appeared, had discovered something big. In the early afternoon of the day she died, she'd sent a text to Renee. *I'm shocked. Right now I'm shaking. I'm sure now I was right! First thing in the morning, I'm going to the police. I don't think I have a choice.*

The first chance that I got, I pulled over, into the parking lot of a hair salon. No way could I drive while I had this conversation. "What was it that she found out?" I asked. "Andy, do we know?"

"Unfortunately not," he replied, his voice coming through the speaker. "And there was another text she sent her sister after that. Hang on. Let me pull it up." There was a brief pause with some rumbling in the background. And then he was back. "Okay, here we go.

This is what she wrote. *Sometimes it's the ones who act so high and mighty who have the most to hide.*"

"Whoa." Elizabeth let out a deep breath.

"Can't they just *ask Renee* what the heck that means?" I asked. "It sounds like it was something they had talked about before. Of course, Renee would know!"

"Well, for some reason, she's decided to keep that to herself," Andy said. "Or at least she didn't say a word about any of those things when she was interviewed. And it's not like we can go back to her now and say, *We have Anna's phone, and this is what it says.* We can't do that unless..."

My heart thumped hard against my chest. Of course they couldn't ask her...if they didn't have her phone. My dirty little secret could be the magic key to wrapping this thing up. But I thought about the way the chief had looked at me that morning. Like I was one more reason he didn't like newcomers. Like I was a dirty fly he wished he could shoo away. And I was terrified. If I walked in with the phone now, they'd all want to know why I'd waited for so long.

Anna's phone, Andy told me, wasn't full of texts or calls that had come in or out. Anna was old-school, keeping her cell mostly in her purse and only using it when something was important. Like me, she'd rather keep up with her friends using gorgeous stationery and nice pens and not spend her days staring at her phone. She would sometimes brighten up my afternoon with a note or card left beside the register with my name written out in her fancy cursive.

"But I did find some stuff that backs up all the things Renee was telling us about the lemon cake," Andy said. "That still seems far-fetched for a motive, but someone seemed to want that thing—and they wanted it real bad." He paused. "And, I have to tell you, some things that I'm seeing that, well, they don't add up."

"Like what?" Elizabeth asked. She took some mints from her purse and offered one to me.

"From what Anna wrote, I get the idea Renee was pushing on her hard to give in to the request, to sell that recipe or share it or whatever. Hang on just a minute." He paused once again. "Here's what Anna texted to her sister a few days before she died. *I know that you're upset. But you have to understand. I made a solemn promise. It was a sacred trust.* And then Renee replied. *Sorry I was whiny. I was having trouble dealing. And you're right about the cake. You always do the right thing, which is what makes you Anna. Stop by after work and check out my new bracelets. I've done something really cool with the antique charms that we found last week at Bernie's. Bring me a cupcake—French vanilla. Promise that you'll grab it now and put it in a box. You know those things get gone. Love you much, my sister."*

Elizabeth scrunched up her brows. "It seems a little odd that Renee would care so much about what her sister did with that recipe."

A silence descended on the car as we thought about it.

Andy was the first to speak. "Someone might have offered to pay a lot of money to get that recipe in their hands. But that would have benefited Anna and not so much Renee."

"Unless," Elizabeth threw out, "it was some family recipe handed down to both the sisters."

Or perhaps the lemon cake was a rare and highly sought-out treat, reserved for the privileged and the royal. (As well as for customers at Anna's, who treasured every bite but didn't have a clue about its pedigree.) But I kept that to myself. It sounded way too crazy.

Andy had a point; there might be money to be made from a recipe as popular as Anna's lemon cake. But the sisters seemed to be in good shape when it came to money. Both the jewelry business and the bakery were doing very well. On the other hand, there was obviously something that had been bothering Renee. *I was having trouble dealing.* Had there been money issues of which we were unaware?

"It could be that someone just got tired of begging Anna for the recipe, so they went through Renee," Elizabeth mused. And I had to admit that made a kind of sense. Renee could be a soft touch while Anna, although she shared her sister's sweetness, could hang tough and hold her own when people tried to take advantage. Journalists, cookbook authors, and charity organizers had been known to plead their cases with Renee when they wanted interviews, appearances, or recipes. And when she had the time, Anna had been happy to comply—with recipes involving chocolate, caramel, or pecan. But never, ever lemon.

"And, as I said before, there weren't a lot of calls—incoming or outgoing," Andy said.

I was not surprised at all. Anna was the only person that I knew who would just as soon leave her phone behind as take it with her.

"You should carry it for safety," I had told her once.

"In Somerset Harbor?" She had laughed. "I might be in danger of running into a snob or an inflated price or two. But my phone won't help me there. Seriously, Rue, it's the safest place on Earth." She had grabbed my hand and smiled. "I know you visit every year, but you should move here!"

Tears welled in my eyes.

Then I thought of something else. "What about that call that came in *after* Anna died, that woman that I talked to? Did you find out who that was?"

Andy knew a little. Her name was Kristie Carpenter, age 32, a stay-at-home mom in Abington, Virginia. She had worked in the fashion industry before she had her children. "So far, I can't find a connection to Anna or Somerset Harbor," Andy said. "But I'm working on it."

After we'd hung up, Elizabeth and I were quiet and exhausted, lost in our own thoughts, as we traveled the winding road that led us back to town. In my head, I tried to make the pieces fit. A sought-out recipe. A drowning years ago that might not have been a drowning. A photo of a place where a pig flew off the roof via a painter's brush. A lady with beguiling eyes who somehow disappeared. A bakery assistant up to something shady. And a troubled sister. I was feeling anxious. There were too many pieces to this awful thing. And the sooner it got solved, the sooner I could breathe.

"Let's make one more stop!" I said. "Let's go to the Harwood's. And if Mel's car is there, we'll stop."

"But the store..."

"It's all fine," I told her. "Ellen said she'd take as many hours as I'd give her. So I'm in no rush—if you're not."

"Fine by me," she said.

Soon, we neared the Harwood house, which sat near the end of a tree-lined street. I loved this part of town, with stately homes that were evenly spaced and fronted by big yards. Then the serene feeling of the neighborhood suddenly was broken by a speeding Lexus that almost careened into my car. *What the heck?* After I jerked at the wheel, pulling us to safety, I glanced at the driver. The man stared ahead intently, his forehead scrunched in fury, a scowl on his face. Beside him sat a startled woman, her eyes grown wide with fear.

I recognized that woman.

"That's Rachel Thorne!" I said.

"They just left the Harwood's." Elizabeth held her hand to her chest and was breathing hard after the near-miss. "They had just pulled out—before that moron very nearly squashed us flat."

Then I noticed something else. A young man was standing at the end of the drive, his hands on his hips, a look of consternation in his eyes.

"That must be the grandson," Elizabeth said. "Might have a lot to say right now! Although I couldn't blame him if he was done with guests."

CHAPTER FIFTEEN

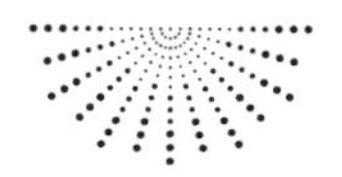

Recovered from our fright, Elizabeth jumped out of the car with a friendly smile. I admired the way that, just like that, she went from scared out of her mind to polished and professional. She handed the young man her card. "Elizabeth Laura Carlisle from Antiquities by Elizabeth. So sorry to disturb you. And this is my associate. May I introduce Rue Collier?"

The young man still looked startled. He straightened up his glasses, which had become askew. He wore a suit and tie and struck me as the type who kept it together almost always. But he had been clearly ruffled by Rachel and her friend. He looked at us and nodded. "Oh, yeah. Elizabeth. Mel said you might be by." He watched the road, still wary. "Oh, and by the way, did you see those people, the people who just left? I swear the woman looked familiar. Like I might have seen her in…what? *People* magazine? Or maybe on the news? But whatever…she's just awful. Both those people were." Then his face turned red. "Oh, man! Please tell me you're not related or that they're some of your best friends. It's just that the guy…" He was breathing hard from the encounter. "He just marches up to me and *demands* to see the items that are left over from the sale. And I told him to get real. It's not like we're in some shopping mall. This is a private home! And the woman acts all sweet at first, then she turns into Freddy Krueger in high heels and red lipstick when she doesn't get her way."

Elizabeth gave him a look of sympathy. "That's because most days, I think she gets her way. That, I am afraid, was Rachel Thorne, who makes her home here in town. An accomplished woman—New York Times bestseller. And obviously used to getting what she wants. I didn't recognize the man. Do you know who he was?"

"Her nephew, maybe? Sheesh! I didn't get his name. Didn't care to ever see the guy again." He stuck out his hand. "By the way, my name is Eddie. I was just packing up some stuff. Would you like to come in?"

"Is this an okay time?" I asked.

"Oh, this is fine," he said. "I would have let those others in if they hadn't come in all entitled. The more the merrier, I say. Cause I'd really love to unload...to *sell* some more...what did you say? Antiquities and stuff. Mel says that it's great stuff! My grandmother always took a lot of pride in all of her collections. She was always decorating. But the thing about it is that the Harwood family has dwindled down to me. And I have a one-bedroom that will barely hold my bed, so a three-hundred-year-old highboy is kind of not my thing."

"I somehow missed seeing that," Elizabeth said, intrigued. "Do you know the finish on the highboy or the maker?" I knew how her mind worked. She was already filling up its drawers with old letters, photographs, and postcards.

"I don't have a clue, but come on in and have a look."

Inside, he had begun to pack things into boxes. The house was up for sale, and Mel would sell the remaining antiquities online or at antique markets, according to Elizabeth. Leaning against the wall was a series of elaborately framed photos of family members through the years, beginning with grim-faced ancestors in old-fashioned clothes and ending with a family portrait of a mother, dad, and tow-headed little boy who I guessed was Eddie. I could tell because the father in the picture had the same large ears and crooked smile as the man who was currently wrapping up Hummel figures and putting them in boxes.

It didn't take me long to find the woman I was searching for in the photographs. With her arresting eyes and pleasant smile, she seemed to draw me to her as if there were a special light that shone out from inside her. She was laughing and looking up at Mr. Handsome from the photos in my store. He had his arms around her waist as if he might pick her up at any minute and spin around with her. The look of adoration in his eyes sent a warm rush through my body. One day, I hoped a man would look at me like that.

Romance had never been one of my favorite genres. But here's one thing I knew. If an author could somehow capture *that* in words, that feeling in that photo, I would curl up in a comfy chair the first chance that I got and just devour that book.

Elizabeth appeared beside me. "Now, *this* photo is my favorite," she called out to Eddie. I admired the way she kept her tone so casual and light. "So much love in their expressions. If you don't mind me asking, who is she, that girl?"

He looked up from his work. "Oh, that's my Great Aunt Margaret. I could tell you stories. But every family has them, right? Famous family stories. Rivalries! Tragedy. Intrigue."

"Tragedy?" I asked. "Does that mean she died young?" I was suddenly more worried about the lady with the long curls and laughing eyes than I was about myself and the cursed text that might well spell my doom. Of course, I had always figured things had not ended well for her.

"It was way before my time. But she drowned in Lake Sinclair when she was probably about the age she might be in that picture." He came to stand beside us. "And okay, here's the thing. Lots of people in my family always felt that she was murdered. Because, according to my grandpa, there was no way she would drown. She had a bunch of brothers, and the whole big group of them would go swimming all the time. My grandpa always said she'd put the boys to shame, that she'd move through the water like a fish."

"Did he talk a lot about his sister?" Elizabeth asked.

"Not a lot," Eddie said. "It still got to him, you know? After all those years. There was a lot of anger there. He was almost sure that somebody followed her that day and held her under. He said he had his reasons but that cops never listen. I tried to ask him more about it when I was a kid. But my mom told me to let it be, not to bring up that old pain."

Just like in the book. The detective part of me was intrigued; another part of me was filled with sorrow. Despite what I'd suspected, I had hoped Eddie would say that our mystery woman had moved to California or

Montana, that she'd been a teacher, artist, fishing guide, had a life she loved.

"Who would have done that to her?" Elizabeth asked.

Eddie shrugged. "According to my grandpa, she was nice to everyone. Everybody loved her is what my grandpa said."

"And this guy in the photo, what became of him?" I asked.

"I think the story was that he moved out West. From what I remember, he was kind of well-known for a while. He wrote advertising jingles. Hey! Like do you remember this?" He sang out a line or two. *Want to run the fastest, make an A on every test? Eat Perfect Yums for breakfast to be your very best.*

I looked back at the picture. I somehow had imagined a different kind of future for him. But he must have been successful. All of my friends and I had eaten that cereal for breakfast as often as our parents would allow. And while fine literature had become the great passion of my life, I knew there was more money to be made in extolling the virtues of Perfect Yums than in writing a gorgeous sentence in a literary novel.

Eddie crossed his arms in front of himself as he looked at the photograph of the laughing couple. "You know, I might take that one with me," he said after a while. "That's what Pop Pop would have wanted—for her to go with me. Mostly I have posters of heavy metal bands, so it's not like this will really fit into my decor. But it's still cool, you know? Can't you kind of tell that she had a sense of humor? I think that if she knew she'd end up on some wall with Iron Maiden posters, she would have laughed and laughed. So, yeah, I think that Great Aunt Margaret is going to Vermont." He picked up the family photo with him as a boy. "And I guess I'll take this too."

I was glad that he was taking that one with his parents. I couldn't bear the thought of somebody's mom and dad being sold for half price to a stranger who kind of liked the frame.

Then I thought about the commune. Anna had seemed intent on learning more about it. Was it important to the story? "Oh, by the way," I said. "I think there was a commune here in your grandparents' time."

"There was," Elizabeth added. "And I have a client with an interest in that kind of thing. Might your grandparents have saved something related to the place?"

"Harmony Farm," he said. "I've heard about the place. I think Aunt Margaret might have even been there briefly. They took in stray cats and dogs—and also horses that were sick or abandoned. That was the draw for her. Supposedly, she was big on taking care of all kinds of creatures. I think my grandma might have had a cookbook from the place. Let me go and look." He stepped into the kitchen, and soon he was back. "Found it! Here you go. It's not much, but it's something. All vegetarian, I think." He made a face.

He handed the book to Elizabeth, and I glanced down at it. The name was written across the cover in green letters. *Good Food From Our Garden and Our Hearts.* The cover featured a scene of children working in a garden. In the background was a wooden building. On the building's roof was a pig in flight.

Elizabeth left her card with him and paid for the cookbook and several other items, including a scrapbook of a tour of Europe taken by the Harwoods long ago. "This is fabulous," she told me. They had saved menus from fine restaurants, which were fun to read, and Lorna Harwood had made extensive notes. *Fish is flavorful but saucy. I wore my new red hat. Waiter tripped and dumped pasta Bolognese into a woman's lap.* She had also pasted in the programs from plays and concerts from the trip. One had been signed by an opera star whose signature would bring a lot of interest, Elizabeth believed.

We also came away with two more boxes of photos, cards, and letters. Those made Eddie smile. "I think that Grandma saved every piece of mail that anybody sent her," he told us.

Elizabeth laughed. "I would do the same, except in this day and age, it's just not as nice to save an email or a text."

I winced at the thought of saving texts. If every single text would go poof and disappear, I would be minus one big headache.

"I'm sure all these cards brought much joy to Mrs. Harwood as the years went by," Elizabeth said. "And now someone else will love them. Why, would you just take a look at these gorgeous stamps..."

I bought a small porcelain frame with room for two photos. Underneath one frame was a painted dog, and underneath the other was a cat. It seemed appropriate now that I had a matching set.

Eddie laughed as he wrapped it up and put it in our bag. "Grandma never did talk Pop Pop into getting her that cat. But I guess she was feeling optimistic when she decided to buy this."

I grabbed the bag, and we bid Eddie farewell, returning back to the car. Arriving back at the shop, we decided that we each would take a box home to explore. I was anxious to dig in, but I was also tired. "What a crazy day," I said. "I know that there might be more answers in that box, but I might be worn out to look for them tonight."

"Oh, Rue," Elizabeth teased. "Are you not at your

best? You must have skipped your Perfect Yums." Then she began to sing. *Want to run the fastest, make an A on every test...*

I interrupted her with a laugh. "See you tomorrow, friend."

Inside the store, things were busy, so I jumped in to help Ellen at the register. It was nearly time to close.

"I'm glad you took some time for you," she said when things slowed down. "I hope you did something great."

"Well, we spent some time in Hampstead."

"Oh, I love the shops in Hampstead!"

"And then when we were almost home, we stopped for some antiquing."

"I hope you found some nice surprises."

"Oh yes, absolutely. Surprises all day long."

CHAPTER SIXTEEN

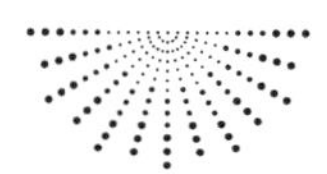

The next morning, I worked a couple of hours before Anna's service, to be held at the First Presbyterian Church of Our Redeemer, two blocks from the store. Elizabeth was at the shop to work the register, and Andy stopped by to walk with me to the church. I was about to burst with the news of Rachel's little scene at the Harwoods' house. But half the town, it seemed, was bunched up on the sidewalks and heading to the church; listening ears were all around.

We got there just in time to snag some aisle seats toward the back. Still tired from the day before (and the nightmarish week), I settled in my seat and let myself be soothed by the rich notes of the organ.

I spotted Jules up near the front. He gazed about him at the crowd, nodding regally to all, like the VIP he thought himself to be. Lined up in the row beside him was the staff from Anna's, all of whom I knew by name. Jane Castleton had begun to weep already, which almost got *me* going.

Andy gave my hand a gentle pat. "She left us way too young," he whispered. He gave my hand a squeeze.

The organ music stopped, and a hush fell over the gathered crowd. *It's about to start,* I thought.

Then I felt a rustling next to me and turned to see a family rush into the row immediately ahead. An elderly couple entered first with a younger man, who kept a steady hand on the woman's elbow while holding tightly to a toddler with his other hand. Following close behind was a woman in her thirties. She had her hair piled high into a messy bun and wore a fashionably cut dress in a shimmery navy blue. She held one child on her hip while she herded three more little ones into the seats ahead.

Once they were somewhat settled, a small girl looked back at me with a shy smile and gave me a little wave. When she caught sight of my tears, she gave me a little pout as if to say that she was sorry I felt sad.

"Felicity Noelle!" the mother hissed as she leaned in close to the girl. *"Toute de suite!* You turn around. It isn't nice to stare." With one hand, she removed a boy's finger from his nose; with the other, she deftly managed to stop the smallest child from fleeing down the aisle. Then she turned to her husband. "We've not been here five minutes and already they exhaust me."

It was her, I thought. I was almost sure that this was the woman who had called Anna's phone. I mouthed the words to Andy.

He sat up straight, alert.

The organ's music started up again. This time it was louder, filling up the church with a majestic sound that once again worked some kind of magic to ease the pounding in my chest. Everybody stood as the family made its way down the aisle. A man I didn't recognize had his arm around Renee. Nervousness shot through me as I watched her lean against him for support. She looked so weak and frail. I was afraid she might collapse and have to be carried out.

The service was short but perfect, with an officiant who'd known Anna half her life. I learned things I'd never known, like that she'd sung in the choir and had perfect pitch. She'd donated day-old goodies to local nursing homes and to underprivileged schools in nearby towns that she would drive to once a week.

After the service, guests were invited to the bakery for the private funeral reception. A fellow chef who catered weddings had volunteered his staff to get the offerings ready. That way, all of Anna's employees could honor her that day as opposed to working the reception.

Andy and I crowded into the full room, where arrays of confectionary treats and sandwiches were set out for the guests. Folding tables were set out as well in the small yard between the bakery and the statue of Adam Stephenson, the founder of our town.

I scanned the room to find the woman with the kids. The woman who I was sure had called Anna's phone. Then a possible name resurfaced from the fogginess that had settled in my brain: Kristie Carpenter. She was about the same age as this woman and was a stay-at-home mom. If she was indeed Kristie, I figured she could be important; she could be the key to finding out what Anna had been so intent on telling the police. *This absolutely must be dealt with,* she had said to "Anna." *There is no telling now what that horrid creature might decide.*

I noticed a crowd that had gathered near the front, and when they parted briefly, I caught a quick glimpse of Renee, whose face looked white and empty. She briefly caught my eye, and the pain that I could read in her expression made me wince. I made my way to the group around her with Andy close behind.

She reached out to embrace me. "Oh, Rue. The last time that I saw you, you and Anna were just having the best time. Don't you remember that? You were having such a laugh—about how you never left the place without cake crumbs on your collar."

"Well, she was right," I said. "I am not known for my grace. And Anna always made me laugh." I looked her in the eye. "Renee, I've been worried sick about you. I just can't imagine. It's beyond belief that Anna isn't here."

Renee just shook her head as tears streamed down her face, and I embraced her once again.

When I finally let her go, Andy extended his hand to her. "Your sister was a treasure. A huge loss, Renee. My deepest sympathies."

Then I heard a familiar voice behind me. "Alexander, no! One cupcake is enough. Now, where did your brother get to?"

I turned to see that the woman's family had found seats at a nearby table while she stood near the buffet. She gripped the hands of two small boys who stood on either side of her, and a determined, steely look was plastered on her face.

Andy glanced toward the table where the rest of the family was gathered. "Oh, by the way, Renee, that family over there?" he asked. "They look so familiar. But I just can't place where I might know them from."

Renee looked confused. "You might be mistaken, Andy. That's Claude and Alice Beaumont with their daughter, Kristie, and her family. Anna worked for them in France. You might have heard her talk about her magic year in Paris. Claude was a big deal there, the top chef at a place that was *tres elite,* as Anna always said." She looked at Claude and smiled. "My sister was extremely lucky. They're good people, Claude and Alice. The Beaumonts are fairly well known if you're into international cuisine. A long line of chefs, all of them legendary. Now, Claude's health is pretty bad from what I understand. They're in Virginia with their daughter. Kristie's husband several years ago was transferred to the States. It was so good of them to come all this way for Anna. They were always good to keep in touch."

Soon the crowd moved in with hugs and sympathetic words for the grieving sister, and we moved away.

"Interesting," I whispered as I walked with Andy to the center of the room.

He nodded, lost in thought. Then he touched my elbow, his mind seemingly having returned to the present moment. "Did I see red velvet cupcakes?"

"I don't know," I said, "but there's a cannoli cake with mascarpone and mini chocolate chips." The mouth-watering descriptions for each gourmet dessert were written in elaborate cursive in cards displayed on the table in front of every dish.

We got in the long line for the buffet, keeping watchful eyes on the esteemed visitors from Virginia.

Kristie's husband by that point had taken the kids outside, where there was room to run off their sugar highs near the founder's statue. Kristie looked almost relaxed as Claude Beaumont nodded his head and chuckled over some story that his daughter was telling him.

I thought about the phone call. Had Kristie told *Papa* yet about the alarming news, or was he still in the dark —like me?

Working our way at last to the front of the line, Andy and I loaded up our plates with triple berry cake, pumpkin bites with cream cheese, grilled ham and gouda sandwiches, and more. More dessert than lunch, but I thought Anna would approve. And this was Anna's day.

"I see a table outside," Andy told me. "Let's try to grab it quick."

We made it to the empty table and set down our plates. "Be right back," I said. "Heading to the restroom."

To my dismay, I noticed that the line for the ladies' room snaked around the corner. But never fear, I thought. I could run next door to the bookshop and be back in a flash. The back door right beside me was marked *Employees Only,* but I slipped out that way, as I sometimes did when I was with Anna. Stepping out behind the bakery, I glimpsed Renee and Kristie sitting at a table on the patio where employees took their breaks. Both women looked upset, and Kristie was a blur as she moved her hands back and forth emphatically to make her point.

I *had* to somehow listen to that conversation. Very quietly, I slipped into a hidden alcove by the door, listening intently. For the sake of anyone who might happen to pass by, I stared down at my phone, as if something on my cell had caught my attention and caused me to stop.

The women were being careful to keep their voices low, but I could hear them fairly clearly.

I heard Kristie speaking first. "Someone could make a *fortune* with that recipe. Some very wealthy people would give almost anything for an authentic version of that cake. It is special to our family, like an heirloom. It was never about profit—not to us, at least. And now an evil man will make his fortune from a thing so close —*grande douleur!*—to my family's heart."

"If he even *has* the recipe. And if he can prove that it's *the one.*"

"The seal! The fleur-de-lis! On the copy Papa gave her. Those who are in the know, who'll pay to get their hands on an authentic copy or an authentic cake—they look for the fleur-de-lis. It is a cake for kings and princes. But also for the nearest and the dearest of our family's special friends. This is our family's gift for them. And it was Papa's gift to Anna—to help her build her business. And now for it to go to Jules, to that disgusting creature. And for the love of money! It was not about the money. Papa always made the cake for love! A cake for *doux amour!*"

"Well, we don't know for sure that he got his hands on the copy that he needed—with the seal for proof. He offered Anna...quite a lot. But Anna wouldn't budge."

"I pray that he did not somehow get it. But, of course, that does not compare with the loss of our dear, sweet Anna. I have cried and cried for days. Well, I must run, Renee. Thirty minutes is the limit before my husband goes crazy with the littles. And yet he wonders why I'm tired when I have them all day long. I must rescue the man."

I put my cell in my purse and moved back toward the door. But I stopped short when I saw Renee, her body bent over the bench, as if she might pass out. I rushed forward to put my hand on her shoulder. "Are you okay?" I asked.

She looked up; her face was white. "Oh, Rue, I just can't stand it."

I eased her toward a chair, and I sat down beside her. "We're all here for you, Renee."

Tears rolled down her cheek. "Heaven help me, Rue," she said.

I reached across to stroke her arm.

Then in the tiniest of voices—one I could barely hear—she said something else. "God forgive me please."

CHAPTER SEVENTEEN

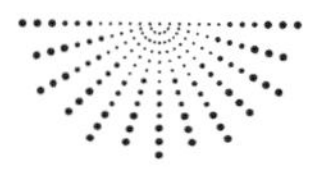

Their words kept running through my mind when I finally made it back to Andy and the table. He sheepishly admitted to sampling some of my desserts. "Just a tiny bite of each!" he said. "You were gone a while, and I was never one to waste a bite of pie."

I was quiet as we ate and visited with some of our friends who stopped by the table to say hi. Then my heart was pounding as Andy walked me to the bookstore, where he said he thought he might run inside to check out our fishing books.

"You okay?" he asked, slowing down when we got to the door. "You don't look so good."

"Something's happened, Andy." I spoke in a low voice. I glanced behind my shoulder to see a lot of people from the funeral heading to their cars. "Let's head back to my office," I told him quietly, "and I'll fill you in."

Inside, Gatsby ambled up to greet us and followed happily behind us as we made our way to the back.

"How was it?" called Elizabeth.

"Moving. Very moving," I called out, not taking time to stop. "It was a perfect service."

Oliver jumped up in my lap as I sank down in the chair behind my desk and told Andy what I'd heard.

His expression went from confused to shock as I relayed the conversation. "I know Anna made some money—and good money too—shipping off those things. But a special symbol of authenticity on *a recipe?* And fortunes to be made? This is just bizarre."

"This cake gets made for weddings of the upper, upper crust—as in royal blood. Oh! And movie stars! Like Adrienne Calloway! You know from that movie, *Under a Glitter Moon!*"

Andy stared. "Well, it *does* sound like a thing that could get a person killed." He leaned back in his chair, resting one hand on his ample belly. "A royal cake? I'll be. This has taken quite a turn."

"Wait! I have a book." I dashed out, followed by Gatsby and his new cat friend, who both seemed to think that I was leading a merry game of chase. Returning, I presented the hardback book to Andy, turned to the proper page. "I found this in the section of the store that Anna had been browsing in right before she died. I was looking for anything, just some kind of hint about what might have scared her enough to write that text." I took a deep, cleansing breath. "This book had been put back hastily, and I found smudges at the bottom of this page, like someone had been lingering on it for quite some time."

Andy read, transfixed.

"At first, I thought *no way* could this be *Anna's* cake," I explained in a hushed voice. "But now I guess that Claude Beaumont, that old guy we just met, is related to the chef who made that first cake in the book. And since Anna worked with Claude that summer, he must have taught her how to make it."

"Taught her how to make it but told her to keep the secret." Andy read on, fascinated. Then he closed the book. "So if he killed her for that little piece of paper, what is Jules's next move? Do you think that he has plans to sell the recipe? Or open up his own place and sell cakes to glitterati at some inflated price?"

"I suspect the latter since we know that he is after that gorgeous Hampstead space. I'm so glad I saved the number of the agent he harassed." I rubbed behind the dog's ear as he put his head in my lap. "I think this afternoon I'll take a little drive and swing by the agent's office."

"Or I can question her myself after I bring Jules into the station for more questions."

"Oh, I feel like a drive." I winked. "It's such a pretty day."

"I have to warn you, Rue. Professionals like that? Most times, they don't talk."

"Andy, you forget—I *was* a professional like that in another life. Let me try to work my magic."

"You go for it then, and I'll talk to Jules. I'll drop the information that we have some knowledge about a certain recipe that might be behind the murder." Andy stood to go. "I'll give him that look that lets the bad guys know that the gig is up. Hopefully, he'll spill, and we'll wrap this baby up."

Then I thought of something that I wished I could forget: Renee's final words to me. The knot inside my chest squeezed around my insides even tighter. "Andy, there's something else," I said. I told him what Renee had said about hoping for forgiveness. I looked at him pleadingly. "She can't have been involved in her sister's death. Andy, there's no way. I'm right. Am I right?"

He frowned. "I'll know more soon, I hope, after I talk to Jules. But I've dealt with a lot of families, Rue, and a lot of deaths. And guilt is just a part of being a survivor.

Things that were left undone, things you wished you'd said. There are a lot of things that she could have meant by that."

I looked in his eyes, trying to determine what he really thought.

As I walked Andy out, we met Ellen coming in.

"Wasn't it the nicest service?" She settled in behind the counter. "I saw you in the crowd."

"I thought it was perfect. Hey, can I ask a favor? I know you've put in extra hours, which I appreciate. This week has just been nuts. But is there any way that you might work till closing? I thought that Elizabeth and I might run back up to Hampstead."

"Absolutely." She straightened a stack of books beside the counter and waved away my look of concern. "It's such a pretty day. Go out and enjoy."

Elizabeth stared at me, confused. "But Rue, I had plans to work on my accounting and do a little..."

"Grab your purse," I said.

She nodded, sensing I was after more than a fancy coffee and a little browsing among high-priced trendy trinkets.

I was showing Ellen a new shipment to unpack when Rachel Thorne breezed in with who I assumed was her husband. Her black shawl fanned out behind her, accented by a shimmery purple overlay and gold dragon pin. She smiled, studying the table dedicated to her works. "I have to say, Marc, it's always a relief to see that some are gone. With every book I put out, I worry that people might lose interest." She spoke in the manner of a woman who thought no such thing.

Marc gave me a sad smile. "We came into town for Anna's service. Such a loss. So young." His quiet dignity stood in contrast to the showiness of Rachel, and the graying near his temples only worked to make his handsome features more distinguished.

When Elizabeth reappeared at the counter with her purse in hand, Rachel smiled at her. "While we were nearby for the service, I thought I'd just run by to peek at that box of items. I did not receive a call, but I'm assuming they're unpacked by now. Marc said he could swing by and pick me up when I'm finished looking. Or he might have a browse in the tobacco shop."

"Well, in fact, I haven't had a chance to unpack and price them," Elizabeth said. "Rachel, I'm so sorry. It's been a little hectic, and we'd discussed before that you'd come in *next* week."

Disappointment—or was it fear?—flashed across the author's eyes. "Well, I don't mean to rush you. But it's research for the next book! And a writer has to write when the muse says write."

Marc put his hand on her shoulder. "I told her that if

the novel is historical, the history won't change. No need to rush the research! But this next book has her raring to get started, which makes me think the subject matter must be fascinating. Not that she ever talks about her works in progress. Writers love their secrets."

I watched as her hand trembled as she touched one of her books. *What was up with Rachel?* The who and why of Anna's murder was falling into place, but Rachel didn't seem to have a role in the sordid tale of Jules and his royal lemon cake. Still, she was hiding something big; of that, I had no doubt.

CHAPTER EIGHTEEN

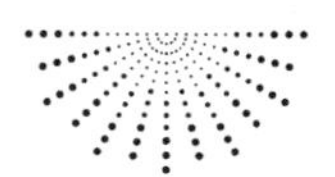

On the way to Hampstead, I gave Elizabeth the details about the conversation that I'd overheard between Kristie and Renee. I left out the part about Renee asking for forgiveness. That part hurt too much; that was the part that scared me most of all.

After a smooth drive with very little traffic, we arrived at the office of Helene Carrington, real estate professional, a few miles outside of downtown Hampstead. Several cars were parked out front, and I really, really hoped that one of them was hers.

As we made our way inside, I took a look around in the heavily air-conditioned office.

As was befitting of the upscale zip code, the lobby was filled with couches covered in expensive fabrics and piled high with silky pillows. A young woman at reception peered into a computer while Helene stood shuffling through some papers at the far end of the desk. I recognized her right away from her headful of blonde curls.

The receptionist looked up and smiled at us. "Good afternoon and welcome. How may I help you ladies?"

I handed her a business card left over from another life. I gave her my best smile, which I still remembered from my days of negotiating deals. I smiled at Helene as well. "I have a client—a professional, very motivated—who would love to buy some space downtown. A place with character and perhaps a bit of history would be the ideal find. Of course, I don't imagine that those kinds of spaces come up for sale very often. And I'm sure that it would be priced accordingly for its premium location—which my client understands. He's pre-approved and ready in case the perfect place might by any chance be available for purchase."

Helene came forward with her hand out. "Helene Carrington," she said. "I'm so happy you stopped by. It just might be your lucky day! I think your client would *adore* the historic Kinsey Building. Built in 1885! It's been a bank and a reception space, and it comes with the original wooden floors and molding. Meticulously cared for and absolutely stunning!"

Soon, we were inside the historic property itself,

having been sprinted away, just like that, in a Mercedes-Benz convertible driven by Helene. Her heavily lipsticked smile had not left her face since she had heard the magic words: *pre-approved and ready.*

"It does look absolutely perfect," I said with a nod. "Any other interest?"

Helene sighed and rolled her eyes, just as I'd hoped she would. "Well there *is* this one guy, but he doesn't seem to be…well, what I mean to say is…I'm not quite sure that he's a fit…*financially*…for this one." Quickly, she put back on her professional demeanor, in which clients were only talked about in the most respectful terms.

I winked and smiled at her. "Believe me, I understand." I cut my eyes to Elizabeth. "As I was saying to my colleague just the other day, the higher the price tag on the property, the more dreamers you attract. The dreamers and the lookie-loos! They think absolutely nothing of wasting all your time."

Elizabeth played along. "Why, one man just last week was insistent on a tour of a two-million-dollar home. And he was just appalled that I would dare to inquire about his financial situation before making an appointment for him to see the house."

"Self-important men," I told Helene with a wink. "Are they not the worst?"

She grabbed me by the elbow and spoke in a quiet voice, her eyes growing wide. "You would not believe the nerve of this one. He was out to rent, not buy, and he thought he'd be approved based on some business plan that he swore would have him and his business all over the TV news. So I should just ignore the fact that he could not begin to pay the first month's rent in his 'current situation.' We would all be very sorry, this guy says to me, that we threw away the chance to be in his esteemed presence!"

"What a loser," Elizabeth said.

"That must be quite a business plan!" I said.

"Oh, it was stupid," said Helene, who dissolved into the giggles. "He thought he was gonna strike it rich because of—are you ready?—a recipe for cake. He said Hampstead would be missing out on the most sought after of ultra-elite desserts." She finally caught her breath. "It's hard to keep your cool sometimes. I would have loved to have told that guy where he could put his cake. Oh, he'll get his comeuppance. But it's just too bad I won't be there to see."

"Did he say where he got this recipe?" I asked. "What a crazy thing."

Helene shook her head, still smiling. "He was talking gibberish. I swear! He said his recipe was special—something about a fleur-de-lis printed on the card. Like why do I even care about the decoration on his copy of a stupid recipe?"

Score! He'd admitted to a witness that he had something valuable of Anna's that did not belong to him. He'd likely killed her for it. And hopefully very soon, he would indeed have a new place that he could call his own, this one behind bars and much less posh than Hampstead.

After our meeting, Elizabeth and I grabbed an early dinner at an Italian place recommended by Helene. "Now we know exactly what that fool was up to," I told her. I dipped my fork into my linguine with clams and white sauce. Even the breeze seemed to be kissed with Hampstead magic on the picturesque patio, which glittered with white lights.

Elizabeth raised her glass in a toast. "Here's to good detective work."

On the drive back, we called Andy and put him on the speakerphone. "How'd it go with Jules?" I asked.

"Not that great." He sighed. "I got him to admit that he'd been after Anna to get the recipe. But he claimed he never got it. He said at one point he thought Renee had come over to his side, but that the sisters were both 'selfish,' as he put it, and didn't want to 'share.' You know, I think we're getting really close to wrapping this thing up. I just need someone who can tell me on the record that he has that recipe."

"No problem, friend. You've got it. I have a name and address," I said.

There was silence on the line. "Rue, sometimes you amaze me. We should put you on the force."

"No thanks. I'll stick with books."

Elizabeth chimed in to fill him in about our day.

"But will this person talk to me?" Andy asked.

I winked at Elizabeth. "She'll talk to you with bells on. I think she'll be more than happy to see the fool go down."

CHAPTER NINETEEN

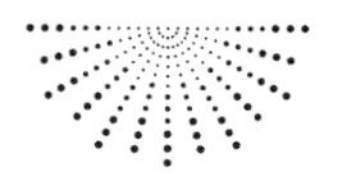

The next day after lunch, while Elizabeth watched the store, I grabbed the book that I had set aside to give Renee along with a box of mint tea. Armed with my two gifts, I headed for her shop.

She looked up, glad to see me. Pumpernickel, the elderly basset hound she had shared with Anna, ambled up to say hello. I was glad that I'd remembered to grab one of the dog treats that I kept at the counter. I held it out to him. "Peanut butter," I said. "This one's Gatsby's favorite."

"I have a project," said Renee as she worked at the counter. "Come tell me what you think."

As I got closer, I could see that she was fashioning a bracelet out of heavy coins and aquamarine jewels whose sparkling color made me think of the sea in a certain kind of light. "Beautiful," I said.

"These are Anna's special coins that she brought back from France." Renee picked up a coin to add to the bracelet. "She said they always made her think of what it felt like to be young in the world's most gorgeous city. I'm making jewelry from her coins. It is what I plan to call my *Belle Soeur* collection."

I smiled, understanding. The name of Renee's new line meant "beautiful sister" in French. "I'll want a piece for sure," I said, reaching out to touch the cool smoothness of the bracelet. I was relieved to see that this new project had brought a little bit of life back to Renee's expression.

"It started as a way to keep Anna close." She fingered a coin in an elaborate silver setting that hung from a chain around her neck. "Then I thought that others might want to have some of the jewelry too. I could spread a little bit of Anna to the people who come in."

"Lucky them." I looked her in the eye. "Tell me how you're doing, and be honest. Is there something I can do? Are you hanging in okay?"

"Not really, but I'm trying." She was silent for a moment. "I just keep getting overwhelmed with all these awful thoughts. Like the fact that Anna deserved a better sister than the one she got."

Pumpernickel settled in against my feet as if my shoes were a pillow. "But Anna just adored you," I said. "Don't you think that for a second."

"The last few weeks were rough. I was not myself, and I pushed her to do something that we both knew was wrong. Thank goodness she didn't listen. Thank goodness Anna did the right thing—as Anna always did. And I apologized."

The recipe, I thought. Had Renee tried to get her sister to sell the recipe to Jules? I could not imagine why. Their finances were fine, and Renee was not a fan of Jules any more than I was.

"I saw a way to get some money that was easy," she continued, fingering the bracelet. "It was easy—but still wrong. And the thing about it was that it involved my health. Or never in a million years would I have ever asked."

My heart felt like it had stopped. "Your health? Are you okay?"

She shook her head. "I haven't told a lot of people. Well, no one except Anna. But I have cancer, Rue. There's hope; there are treatments, but they're experimental and not covered by insurance. But Anna was determined; she said we'd find a way. She said we'd plan a benefit, do something, do a lot of things…but not the thing I asked."

I gave her a hug. "And now *we* can find a way—all of your friends in town. You're not alone in this."

My phone buzzed, and I looked down to see a text from Andy. *We've just arrested Jules for Anna's murder. Call me right away.*

"Hey, look, I've got to run," I said. "Dinner? Tomorrow night? I think we both could use a girls' night."

She smiled. "Count me in. First, stop by the shop and pick out your favorite coins and stones. I'll get started on a necklace. Anna would have liked that." She sighed. "I'm trying so hard, Rue, to focus on good things like this. If they'd just make an arrest, I think I could make some progress."

I nodded. "Hang in there, Renee. I'm betting that they'll have some news for you real soon."

I rushed to the bookshop. Inside the store, I smiled at the customers as I made my way back to my office. The pets followed eagerly, as they always did. I sat down at my desk, and Andy answered right away. I settled back against my office chair. "Tell me everything," I breathed.

It hadn't taken long for Jules to confess once Andy told him what the witness was prepared to say: that Jules had Anna's recipe and that he planned to use the stolen property for financial gain. There had been no signs of remorse. Jules's arrogance had, in fact, remained intact. The recipe belonged not just to Anna but to the world, he'd said—and to a "master businessman" who could use it for great things. Andy sighed as he told the story. "*Belonged to the world,* my foot," he said. "All this guy cared about was how much dirty money he could stuff into his pockets."

Apparently, Jules had offered to buy the recipe once he'd learned of its special provenance and the demand for the cake among moneyed clients. Although Anna had usually been discreet, he had overheard the details in whispered conversations that she'd had with Renee. He had been appalled that Anna refused to advertise the history behind her bestselling cake. She could have made a fortune. But Anna had insisted that she had made a promise to a friend that the information would never be revealed.

When Anna had refused to sell, he would sometimes stay late at the bakery to search for a copy. Then when that plan failed to produce results, he'd sit outside the bakery on the bench to watch the apartment where Anna lived, hoping to sneak inside her place to grab her copy while she was away.

"*Someone* found a copy," I said, remembering the recipe discovered on the sidewalk.

"That's what she handed him at first when the no-good scoundrel held the knife up to her throat. But that's not the one he needed. He needed an 'official' copy that was handed down from a proper source. Which she finally gave the guy—before he killed her so she wouldn't talk."

Had she seen him lingering on the bench watching where she went? Had he threatened her before—enough to inspire a text? *Leaving bookstore now. Feeling terrified. I don't want to be alone here.* She must have been afraid to walk to her apartment with Jules waiting right outside. But why had she not said so? She could have gone with me to my place. Why put herself in danger?

I came out of my office with the two pets trailing happily behind me like a small parade. With no customers around, I told Elizabeth the news. I should have felt relief, but something felt unfinished; something didn't fit.

Elizabeth agreed. "I get that it was likely that she was scared of Jules. But she was also scared of something else, something in that stuff I bought at the Harwood sale.

Tonight we'd search the boxes. Anna had known something; Rachel had known it too. It had terrified one woman and made another very anxious to see what other secrets might be packed away in all of that old stuff.

I could hardly wait for the workday to be over.

CHAPTER TWENTY

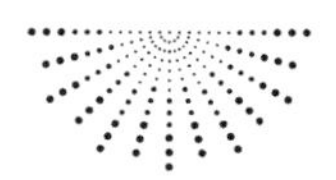

That night, I poured myself a glass of Chablis and dug into the stuff from the Harwood house. Elizabeth was going through the other boxes at her place.

I pulled out an envelope of photos. More of them than not featured Great Aunt Margaret, which was really no surprise. She had the kind of beauty that drew a person to her, and of course, whoever held the camera might gravitate to her. In one especially striking picture, she sat beneath the spreading branches of an oak.

"You should see the necklace that she's wearing in this picture," I called out to Elizabeth, who I had on speakerphone. "It's this artsy looking star. I want one of those! The woman had good taste."

"Sometimes it's amazing how we think alike. I

noticed that same necklace in another shot," Elizabeth said. "I asked Mel if he had it; I would have snapped it up, and Mel checked in with Eddie. Apparently, our lady had it on the day she died. And it must have fallen off—somewhere in Lake Sinclair."

But it looked familiar too. Was that design, that brand, still being sold somewhere after all those years? It looked like a one-of-a-kind sort of piece, possibly handmade by the artistic Margaret.

We worked awhile in silence with only the sound of a fierce wind that had started up outside. Sifting through a stack of greeting cards, I noticed that many of them featured brides and grooms, along with wedding bells. *Congratulations, Margaret,* Mr. and Mrs. Dan Ballew had written in a card. *What a stunning bride you'll be.*

"Engagement cards!" I told Elizabeth. "Engagement cards for Margaret. I think she married Mr. Handsome." But then the next cards were embossed with messages of a more somber tone. Gold words across the front of one expressed *Deepest Sympathy.* Inside was a message written in black cursive: *So sorry for the loss of your precious Margaret.* I compared the postmarks on the envelopes. Just a few short weeks separated the engagement cards with those sent to the family in bereavement. Sadly, the effervescent Great Aunt Margaret never got to be a bride.

The search became less lively after that. Although we already knew there was no happy ending, our hearts still broke just a little.

Ten minutes—and many cards and photos later—Elizabeth broke the silence. "Here's the flying pig again," she said. "And more pictures of the couple. They're working at the commune, which is where they met, I guess."

Five minutes later, she updated me again. "Found her obituary! Pasted on a scrapbook page."

I stopped what I was doing and put down a stack of postcards. Something was nagging at me in the corner of my mind. "Someone drowned that girl in Rachel's book the same week she got engaged. The groom's old girlfriend was behind it. She talked a neighbor into killing the character in the book. They made it look like she had drowned, and no one was ever charged. And, Elizabeth, think about what Eddie told us. His father never thought his sister's death was an accident." Had a real-life murder found its way into the book? Was that why Rachel freaked out when she saw Margaret's picture and the items from the commune where Margaret and her fiancé lived? Rachel might be hiding the identity of a real-life killer.

"I wish we knew the name of the fiancé," Elizabeth said. "And the person he was dating before he fell in love with Margaret."

"Be right back." I ran to get my laptop. I settled against the cushions of the couch and searched online for *famous jingle Perfect Yums.*

Three paragraphs into the first story that I read, I sat up a little straighter and I gasped out loud.

The famous jingle for the brand, arguably better known than the cereal itself, was penned by Marcus Thorne, who later married Rachel Thomas Thorne, famed for her best-selling thrillers.

"Poe's raven in an apple tree!" I called out to Elizabeth.

"What?"

I read her what I'd found.

"Do you think..." Her voice trailed off.

"That would explain why she was anxious to see what might be in that stuff," I said.

Another article had a longer biography with more information on Marcus and Rachel Thorne. *The two met in their Massachusetts high school, where they quickly paired up and became the most popular couple in their class. They have been together ever since except for a brief break in their twenties while he spent time in a commune and she in a writer's colony.*

Then it hit me with a force that made me almost lose my breath. I had seen that necklace not that long ago. Rachel had been wearing it in the bookshop the day after Anna had been murdered.

I hung up with Elizabeth and called Andy, breathing hard.

"Well, if it's not the ace detective," he said by way of greeting. "You were brilliant, Rue. It's not every day that my favorite bookstore owner leaves her paperbacks behind to go out and catch a killer."

"Two killers, Andy. Two. I'm pretty sure it's two."

"What? Rue, what do you mean? Do you think that Jules had help?"

"No." I took a deep breath. "I think that Rachel Thorne killed her husband's former fiancée back when she was a girl."

I could tell that I had left him speechless for a moment.

"Well, that seemed to come from nowhere," he said after a while.

"Can you just come over here?" I asked.

"On my way."

CHAPTER TWENTY-ONE

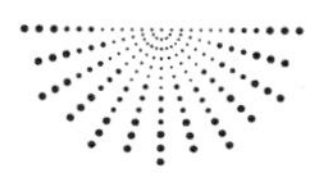

When Andy brought her in the next day, Rachel, in a sea of tears, admitted to her role in the murder that became the subject later of her first published book. As somewhat of an expert in clues and the nailing of suspects, she must have known that the game was up when Andy sat across from her and laid out his case: the "accidental drowning" in the book that exactly matched the demise of her former rival—along with her possession of the necklace that Margaret had been wearing on the afternoon she died.

Rachel had paid a neighbor, long since dead, to follow Margaret to the lake and drown her. The boy had brought the necklace back as proof, and Rachel sometimes wore it as a souvenir of what she called her "victory in love."

"I would call it something else," Andy told me, frowning. "If you have to drown a girl to get a man, how *in love* could he be?"

"He *was* in love," I said. "Just not in love with her."

Sales of Rachel's thrillers soared in the weeks that followed, when TV stations from all over descended with a force into our normally quiet square. I had to bring in extra help just to man the phones. Readers from across the country—and in fact, the world—clamored for special autographed editions of the book that told the story of a murder in which the author played a part. Specifically, readers wanted copies from the Seabreeze Bookshop, because our books were special. Along with Rachel's signature, the copies that we shipped had the special seal that my gran had long ago designed for Rachel's books. *From Somerset Harbor, Massachusetts. Seaside Home of Rachel Thorne.*

The increased demand, of course, was no surprise to me. Anticipating trends and stocking shelves accordingly is all part of the job. Which is the reason I asked Andy to let me put in a call to our "esteemed" author before he brought her in for questions. So just before our most famous citizen was locked away for murder, I had her sign every copy of a Thorne book that I had in stock. I also got her signature on some special bookplates. I'd paste those into the extra copies of *Death is Not a Stranger Here* that I would order later.

To get Rachel to come in, I made up some tale about an expected surge of tourists in the coming months. "And you know that they'll all want an autographed Rachel Thorne," I told her with a smile.

I kept it kind of vague, but it didn't matter. Flatter an author with praise, and they'll pull out the pen and sign their books with no questions asked.

Two weeks after her arrest, the proceeds from the books were still pouring in—enough I hoped to pay for the experimental treatments that the doctors thought held promise for Renee. I was profiting, I supposed, from murder. Not a pleasant thought! But it was Margaret's murder, and I was almost certain I knew what she would say. *You go, girl,* she'd tell me. *Let's do it for Renee.*

Renee had eventually confided more about her sister's final days. Anna had apparently begun to have suspicions about Rachel after reading her early work and seeing things in Elizabeth's collection that linked the real-life murder to the murder in the book. She was planning to take the information to the cops right before she died.

That bit of information suggested that Jules might have had more motive than a lemon cake recipe for killing Anna. Perhaps he hadn't told Andy the entire truth in an attempt to protect the esteemed author, who had likely paid him to do her dirty work for her—like she'd paid her neighbor to kill Margaret many years ago. But regardless, both Jules and Rachel were now behind bars, justice finally served.

"I was trying to decide if I should tell the cops myself since she couldn't do it," Renee told me one night over dinner. "But I was in bad shape then, and she didn't give me details about everything she found."

No one was more stunned by the revelations than Rachel's husband Marc, the handsome suitor from the pictures. (I'd been selling books to Mr. Handsome all along without knowing it was him.)

"I had a good life with Rachel," he told one TV station, "but my one true love was Margaret. I never forgot her. Ever."

After things had settled down, I was rubbing Oliver's white tummy when a young couple strode into the store. The girl exploded into a series of very high-pitched coos when she saw the cat. "I was hoping that you'd keep him," she told me, rushing toward the counter.

The boy watched the playful cat and grinned. "Yeah.

That's really cool. The kitten has a home! Guess he walked into the right place after all."

"I suppose he did," I said, recognizing the young couple who'd been in the store the night that Anna died.

The boy headed toward the graphic novels, but soon he was back. "You know, this is really weird," he said. "The last time we were here, that time we found the cat, we also found some lady's purse. And now some other person seems to have left something of theirs as well? This phone looks ancient." He looked down at the phone with an air of disapproval at the make or model.

I took the phone and smiled. "I'll just keep the phone right here, and maybe they'll be back."

If not, there was no way I was gonna touch that phone. If that phone could tell me who the owner was—or any juicy secrets—I wasn't gonna look. Lesson given, lesson learned.

Instead of snooping on the phone, I'd give my pets some extra treats. I'd create some new displays with books of local interest, including some new cookbooks that had just come out from two local restaurants. Samples! We'd serve samples. I'd call the authors right away and see if they liked the idea of serving samples from their books at the entrance to the store. A thing like that could make their sales go up and maybe even double.

The jingle of the bell caused me to look up from my orders. It was Larry Mullins from the boat rentals operation on Lexington and Jones.

"Larry, great to see you." I moved toward the door to greet him. "We just got in a new science fiction novel that's been getting lots of buzz. Want me to show it to you?" Larry could devour a science fiction book in a single day if it was the off-season or if rainy weather meant a slow day for his rentals.

"Awesome," he told me. "You know what I love to read."

It felt like a normal day. I loved days that were normal.

I handed him the book, already contemplating what I'd have for lunch.

The next time the bell tinkled, I looked up to see Renee.

"I have to cancel next week for the movies," she told me, smiling shyly. "I'll be in Boston—getting treatment."

"Renee, that's great," I said. With sales from Rachel's books plus a fundraiser at the church, I knew that a lot had been collected. But with the treatments going for a price that was frankly shocking, I didn't think that she was close.

She could read my mind.

"I got a call from Kristie," she explained. "And, well, it looks like I'm all set."

Before she died, it seems that Anna had talked with a few of her connections about some ideas she had to raise money for her sister. She'd asked Kristie what she thought about a cookbook that included recipes from well-known chefs. Kristie said she'd think about it. Then with everything that happened, Kristie had just forgotten. Understandable.

Then not too long ago, Renee had received a call. Kristie had remembered that Renee was in need of funds—lots and lots of funds. It was the kind of money that was hard to get. Unless you can sell four or five lemon cakes for the kind of money one can get for the most elite of wedding cakes, fit for a king or queen. Which is what Kristie had done.

For the next five cakes that were sold, the proceeds went into the fund that the town had set up for treatments for Renee.

For the first time in a long time, I thought Renee looked happy.

A sweet ending after all.

# # #

Thank you for reading! Want to help out?

Reviews are crucial for independent authors like me, so if you enjoyed my book, **please consider leaving a review today**.

Thank you!

Penny Brooke

ABOUT THE AUTHOR

Penny Brooke has been reading mysteries for as long as she can remember. When not penning her own stories, she enjoys spending time outdoors with her husband, crocheting, and cozying up with her pups and a good novel. To find out more about her books, visit www.pennybrooke.com

Made in the USA
Columbia, SC
11 January 2024

30296884R00093